MURDER IN THE FORBIDDEN CITY

MURDER IN THE FORBIDDEN CITY

A QING DYNASTY MYSTERY BOOK 1

AMANDA ROBERTS

Red Empress Publishing
www.RedEmpressPublishing.com

Cover by Cherith Vaughan
www.shreddedpotato.com

ALSO BY THE AUTHOR

Fiction

Threads of Silk

The Man in the Dragon Mask

The Qing Dynasty Mysteries

Murder in the Forbidden City

Murder in the British Quarter

Murder at the Peking Opera

The Touching Time Series

The Emperor's Seal

The Empress's Dagger

The Slave's Necklace

Nonfiction

The Crazy Dumplings Cookbook

Crazy Dumplings II: Even Dumplinger

1

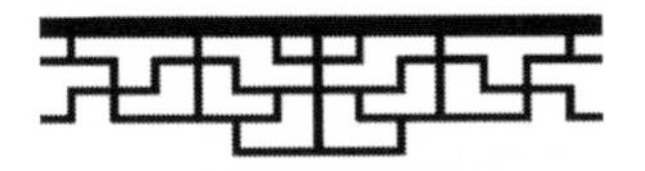

The empress, high up on her dais, wept uncontrollably. The baubles dangling from her elaborate hairdo quivered as she hid her face in her trembling hands.

The dead girl, one of the empress's ladies-in-waiting, was lying on a long table in front of Inspector Gong. The investigation has already been botched beyond solving since the girl had been moved from the scene of the crime. Who knew how many people had trampled through the scene itself. The eunuchs had probably worked quickly to clean up the mess. The other men present, the ministers and advisors, had no words to comfort the empress. Everyone of importance was there except for the emperor himself. Such horrors were not appropriate for a child.

"Who did this?" the empress shrieked. "I demand to know!"

The room stayed silent as she resumed her crying. The empress, young as she was, was a formidable force, yet the inspector knew the killer would not make himself, or herself, known just because the empress demanded it. This was one situation where the empress was not going to get her way.

"Your Majesty," Inspector Gong finally said, "may I have a closer look at the body?"

The empress nodded her consent. "Just don't touch her!" she yelled.

"Of course," the inspector replied, even though her demand was ridiculous. How could he get a complete understanding of what happened if he couldn't examine the body fully? He approached the girl and kneeled down next to her. She had been stabbed several times in her neck and chest, her qaopao ripped open where the knife slashed through the beautiful fabric. Dark splotches of blood stained the light blue satin. The blood was dark, almost black. Even though blood typically darkened over time, it seemed unnaturally dark. Her hands were bloody as well and showed evidence of a struggle. Someone else's blood, perhaps. Her hair was a mess and her shoes were gone. She had fought back and most likely tried to flee from her attacker. Her jaw was tightly clenched and her eyes closed. Her death had been frightening and painful.

"What was her name?" the inspector asked in a loud clear voice so all could hear. He stood straight and crossed his arms as he looked around the room.

"Lady Yun," one of the eunuchs replied.

"How old was she?" he asked.

"Fifteen, sir."

The inspector grunted. Fifteen. And she was beautiful, even in death. The long eyelashes of her closed eyes lay upon her pale cheeks.

"Who were her family?" he asked.

"She had no male relatives," the eunuch replied.

"She was an orphan?" the inspector asked.

"No, sir. She has a mother, but she is sickly. She was primarily cared for by her brother and sister-in-law until her brother's death. Her sister-in-law is her guardian, but the girl had been living here at the Forbidden City for the last year."

"I'll need to speak to her sister-in-law," he said. "Has she been informed yet of the girl's death?"

"No, sir."

"Good, I want to be the one to tell her. I need to see her reaction."

"Whatever you need," the empress finally spoke up, "it shall be yours. You must find who did this."

"I need to see where she was killed, and speak to all the other ladies of the Inner Court who knew her."

The room gasped, and the empress stared at him in shock. The men began to murmur and argue among themselves.

"That is not possible," one of the men said loudly, pointing a finger at the inspector. "No man can be allowed in the Inner Court. It is for the women's protection."

"Protection?" the inspector asked. "One of the empress's own ladies was murdered inside the very walls of the Forbidden City. Make no mistake; if someone could kill this girl, no one here is safe. Look at her hands, the stab wounds. She must have screamed. How could no one have heard her? I must be allowed to inspect every aspect of this crime if any member of the royal family wishes to feel safe in their own home again."

The inspector knew he was making things worse. There was no evidence that the killer would strike again or that the empress or child-emperor were in danger, but unless he were allowed behind the sealed doors of the Inner Court, he would never find the killer. If he had to frighten the empress out of her wits to achieve his goal, he would do so.

The room erupted in yelling and arguments. The empress was no longer crying, but was looking around the room with her large, dark eyes.

"Inspector," she finally said, silencing the room. "Are you saying you think *I* could be in danger?"

"I do not know, Your Majesty," he said. "But I can rule nothing out. I do not know if Lady Yun was the target of the killer's rage or if she only got in the way. I do not know if the killer has fled or if he, or she, is within this very room." Another round of gasps followed. "What I do know," he continued, "is that this investigation should be the court's priority, and to do my job properly, to bring the killer to justice, I need to be allowed into the Inner Court of the women."

The empress opened her mouth to speak, but she was interrupted by a court minister by the name of Song. "No!" he said firmly. "It is forbidden and improper. You cannot violate the sacred space of the women's quarters. To do so would be as violating the women themselves."

"Minister," Inspector Gong nearly laughed. "Investigating a murder would hardly be the same as taking a woman to bed...at least in my case." Several of the other men laughed.

"This is no laughing matter," Minister Song erupted. "If you cannot do your job from outside of the Inner Court, then you are not worthy of your title and should be stripped of your rank and salary immediately!"

"Now, see here, Minister..." the inspector began.

"I agree," another minister interrupted. "Is his job worth doing if it violates the integrity of the empress?"

Several other men spoke up in agreement.

"Enough," the empress finally said, her voice clear and even. The room went quiet. She was calm now. Even her hands were steady. "I agree this case should be of the utmost importance. My own safety and the safety of the emperor rely on it."

"Thank you, Your Majesty," Inspector Gong replied.

"However," she continued, "we cannot allow this killer, whoever he is, disrupt our lives and the way things are done. Tradition and court procedure are at the very center of the throne and the country. I have to agree with the ministers. You cannot be allowed to enter the Inner Court, Inspector."

"So you will allow a killer to go free?" he asked. "Allow a murderer to perhaps roam your very halls?"

"No," she said. "You will find the killer. And you will do so quickly to ensure that my son is safe. You will have everything you need at your disposal, but you will do so from *outside* the Inner Court."

With that, the empress stood to leave. All of the men immediately dropped to their knees and kowtowed before her. She exited from a side door, followed by her entourage of ladies, maids, and eunuchs. After the door closed behind her, the men all stood and gathered around the dead body of the girl or in their usual cliques.

Inspector Gong motioned to one of the eunuchs who had remained. "You, make sure the body is taken to Dr. Xue in Qifeng District. He will know what to do." The eunuch bowed and went to find some other eunuchs and a cart to make the arrangements.

"Do you really think the imperial family could be in danger?" Prince Kung, the empress's brother-in-law and the emperor's regent—in name only—asked the inspector.

"I don't know," the inspector said with a sigh as he reached down and brushed a loose hair from Lady Yun's face. "I don't know anything at this point. If I can't talk to the other women, if I can't see where she was killed...how am I supposed to investigate this crime from the outside?"

The prince smiled and slapped Inspector Gong on the back. "I am glad I am not in your shoes."

"Usually I say the same thing of you," Inspector Gong smiled back. "I would not want to battle with her on a daily basis. Today was enough."

"She's not so bad once you get to know her," the prince replied.

"And what about her?" he asked, motioning to Lady Yun. "Did you know her well?"

"Those girls all look the same to me," he said. "They come and go so quickly. They are all the most beautiful girls from the best families. They serve the empress for a couple of years, get married, leave, and new ones take their place. Why bother learning their names?"

"Well, someone knew who she was."

"What do you mean?" the prince asked.

"This kind of violence against a woman, a girl, shows a lot of anger. Who would lash out in this kind of rage at a girl like that?"

"You don't know court life," the prince said. "It's... competitive. The women all compete for attention, for money, for position..."

"Sounds like a good place to start, but I'm stuck out here."

"What will you do?" the prince asked.

"What about her guardian? Her sister-in-law?"

"I'll talk to Te-hai, the head eunuch. He should know all about her."

"Thanks," the inspector said. At least he might find out something about the girl's past if he talked to the family.

2

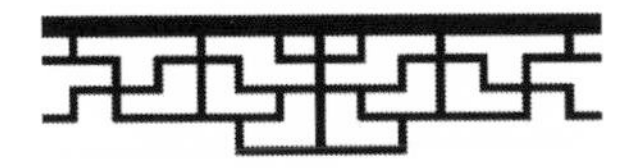

"In the eleventh year of the Xianfeng Emperor, the emperor died," the little girl recited from her book.

"And where did he die?" Lady Li asked.

"At the hunting palace in Jehol," her oldest daughter answered.

"Very good. And why was he there?"

"Because the White Devils drove him out of Peking."

"That's right," Lady Li answered. "We tried to hide in the Summer Palace first, the most opulent palace in all of China, but the foreign barbarians chased us out and they burned the Summer Palace to the ground, after they stole all they could carry first."

"Were you scared, Mama?" her other, younger, daughter asked.

"Of course! We thought the foreigners were going to ride up behind us and hack us to bits with their big swords."

"But they didn't," the older girl said.

"No, they didn't. After the emperor died, with the help of Prince Kung, the empress was able to broker a peace with the foreign powers and they allowed her to return to the Forbidden City."

"With the little prince!" the younger daughter piped up.

"Yes, with the little prince, who was now the little emperor! But he was too small to rule, and he still is. So while he grows up, we have a beautiful and benevolent empress to rule instead."

"I want to see the empress," the older girl said.

"I am sure someday you will," Lady Li replied. "Your auntie, Yun Suyi, is serving her now. I served her. And when you are old enough, she will probably send for you."

"That would be amazing!" the older girl said, sliding off her mother's lap. "To live in the palace! And have people wait on you all day! And eat the best foods and wear the best clothes!"

Lady Yun could have told her daughter that living in the palace was hardly fun or easy. The ladies who waited on the empress had to rise at the hour of the rabbit to help her wash, dress, apply her makeup, and do her hair all before breakfast. Then they had to stand to the side while she ate, and only after she was finished would they be allowed the leftovers. They had to stand at her side at public audiences, which often lasted for hours. They had to keep the empress entertained. They even had to wipe her backside after she used the porcelain bowl. They could not rest until after the empress was asleep, often in the latest hours of the night. It was not a glamorous life. But she did not tell her daughter this, not now. She was still young, only six. She had time to live in a dream before growing up. Her other daughter was only four and still her baby. Probably her last.

As a widow, Lady Li did not entertain the idea that she would marry again and have more children. She was expected to honor her late husband for the rest of her days.

To take another man to bed, even a husband, would dishonor her. Considering the large fortune her husband left behind, she could be commanded to marry again by the empress, especially if the empress needed to buy someone off. If she married, her new husband would control her estate and could spend her money as he saw fit. But if she didn't marry, she could eventually divide her holdings evenly between her daughters. What a dowry that would be! They could marry anyone she wanted, even princes, perhaps even the emperor.

Lady Li shook herself out of her daydreaming and ordered the girls to their embroidery work. "That's enough studies for now," she said. "Go sit with Concubine Swan and have her help you with your stitches."

"Yes, Mama," the girls said as they ran off.

Lady Li then went about her own afternoon chores, overseeing the dinner preparations, ordering new bolts of satin, silk thread, and animal pelts to begin work on new winter clothes, and going over the household accounts. Lady Li enjoyed her busy, yet relaxed, life. Without a husband to kneel to, Lady Li was free to run her household as she wanted and did not have to worry about making someone else happy. Not that she was glad of her husband's death; she was merely indifferent to it. She did, however, mourn the fact that she never had a son.

After three years of marriage and two daughters, her husband had taken on a concubine to help increase their chances of having a boy. Concubine Swan got with child quickly, and they all celebrated. As the head wife, any child born to any of her husband's women would be considered her own. She would take the lead in raising him and he would call her mama. But after her husband's sudden death, Concubine Swan miscarried. Lady Li mourned three times: once for her husband, once for Concubine's Swan's child, and once for all the children she would never have. It had been three years since her husband's death. She should have arranged a new marriage for Concubine Swan, but since she was used property and had lost a child, no man of quality was willing to accept her. If Lady Li pressed the issue, she could probably find a man to take Concubine Swan away, but in truth, she would miss her. Concubine Swan was a sad and lonely woman. At least Lady Li had a considerable fortune, a household to run, and two lovely daughters. Concubine Swan had nothing and no future, and she was only nineteen years old. Lady Li had great empathy for Concubine Swan and enjoyed her company as they did embroidery work together or shared neighborhood gossip. She would keep Concubine Swan in her home for as long as Concubine Swan wished to stay.

Lady Li did not realize just how lost in thought she was until she felt a hand on her shoulder.

"My lady?" she finally heard her eunuch, Bai, say.

"Oh, forgive me. I was dreaming," Lady Li said.

"You have a lot on your mind, my lady?" Eunuch Bai replied.

"Nothing more than usual," she replied. "Did you need something?"

"Forgive me," he said, "but there is a man here to see you."

"A man?" Lady Li replied, surprised. "And he wants to see me? Why? Who is he?"

"He said his name is Inspector Gong."

"Could he not talk to you?" she asked.

"He refused, my lady. I pressed him several times and warned him about how improper he was acting, but he insisted. He said he comes with orders from Prince Kung himself."

"Prince Kung?" she asked, sitting up. This was all extremely out of the ordinary. Men and women in China lived very separate lives, rarely interacting if they were not of the same household or family. Since Lady Li was the head of her own household, she did have more interactions with men than most women, but it was still quite limited. If she required any dealings with men, she usually did so through Eunuch Bai.

But she had never been in a situation like this before. What would an investigator want with her? And with the authority of Prince Kung? She knew Prince Kung from her own years at the Forbidden City and through her family connections. If the prince needed something, why did he not come to her himself or order her to appear at court? Something was very wrong. Had something happened to the empress? Or her sister-in-law, Suyi?

"Where is he?" she asked.

"I have him sitting in a room near the south gate," he said. "Madam Ling is serving him tea."

"Help me dress," she said. "Quickly."

Since Lady Li rarely had visitors and left her home even less often, she was not presentable for company. She was wearing a very plain chaopao of dark blue with a simple trim, her hair was plaited, and she was wearing flat-soled shoes. Eunuch Bai helped her pull out a more elegant light blue chaopao with butterfly embroidery and a more elaborate trim. He didn't have time to do her hair in the batou style, so he arranged it in a plaited bun and decorated it with jade pins. As a widow, she was forbidden from wearing makeup, but she could not resist using a little coal on her eyelashes and around her eyes and adding a little color to her cheeks and lips. Before stepping out the door, Eunuch Bai helped her step into a pair of high pot-bottom shoes, as was the style for Manchu women since they didn't bind their feet. She needed help balancing and walking for the first few steps, she was so out of practice with wearing them, but after a few steps, her body recalled the swaying rhythm necessary and she was able to make her way to the front room where this Inspector Gong was waiting.

As soon as she passed through the doorway, Inspector Gong stood. Lady Li had no idea what he was expecting, but he seemed surprised to see her. He smiled and stuttered as he introduced himself.

"I am Inspection Gong...Inspector Gong!" he said as he stepped forward and gave a respectful bow.

Madam Ling, Lady Li's old housekeeper, laughed as she exited the room.

Lady Li kneeled slightly and inclined her neck just so. She was being polite, but her station did not require her to show any respect to this stranger. She did not make eye contact with him as she walked toward the table and sat in the chair opposite his.

"I hope you enjoyed your tea while you were waiting. You will forgive my delay. I had no notice of your coming," she said.

"Forgive me, Lady Li," he said as he sat down and poured her a cup of tea, "but there was no time to send a notice. I had to speak with you on a matter of grave importance."

Lady Li looked the inspector in the face for the first time. His eyes were hard and serious and his jaw was set firm. He wasn't exaggerating, and her heart began to beat quickly.

"Then, please, state your business," she said.

He glanced at Eunuch Bai. "My news is quite sensitive," he said quietly. "May we speak privately?"

"Certainly not!" Lady Li replied firmly, and at a normal volume. "You shouldn't be speaking to me at all, let alone privately. Now, state your business or leave my home."

Inspector Gong set his teacup down and looked into Lady Li's eyes. "Lady Li, I am sorry to inform you that your sister-in-law, the Lady Yun, is dead. She was murdered."

Lady Li's eyes widened and her hands shook. She could not have heard him correctly. "What did you say?" she asked.

"I am sorry to be so blunt, madam, but it is true. I am sorry for your loss."

Lady Li tried to put her cup down gently, but instead she dropped it as she gripped the table, the cup shattering and tea spilling on her chaopao. "Bai!" she wailed as he ran to her side. "It's not true! Tell me this monster is lying!"

"My lady...my lady," was all he could stammer as she gripped his arms and tears started to fall. Eunuch Bai did his best to hold her upright as she began to crumple into herself.

"Lady Li," the inspector said gently. "I need you to be calm. I need your help."

Lady Li looked at him through watery eyes, but she could not see. She could not do this again. Suyi! Her dear Suyi! The girl was like her sister, her friend, and a daughter all together in one beautiful person. Such life, such promise. She couldn't breathe. She had to get out. She did her best to stand, but she couldn't walk in those stupid pot-bottom shoes. She kicked them off and wandered toward the doorway. She leaned on the doorjamb and vomited in the hallway.

3

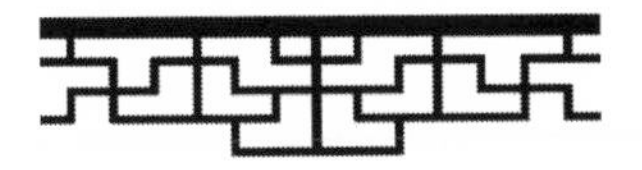

Inspector Gong had told many people about the death of a loved one before, but he was never prepared for the reaction. He had discovered that everyone grieved differently. Some people cried, some people got angry, some people would sit in stunned silence. Some people even laughed. But every reaction told him something. It was clear to him that Lady Li was in shock. She had no idea that her sister-in-law had been killed. He was relieved at this, but the level of her grief was a bit surprising to him. It was uncommon for a woman to have so much affection for her husband's family. When a woman married, she had to leave her own family and join his. She was usually considered an outsider in a new clan, a lone horse. Rarely was a woman ever truly accepted as a part of her husband's family. Maybe the fact that Lady Li was a widow, and such a young one at that, had something to do with how close she was to her sister-in-law.

Eunuch Bai had helped Lady Li from the room, sending Inspector Gong many dirty looks along the way, to help her clean up and compose herself. Madame Ling returned, tears in her eyes as well, and had asked the inspector to leave, but he refused. He still wanted to talk to Lady Li. If he could talk to her in her grief, her answers would be raw and honest.

Nearly an hour later, Eunuch Bai came back. "I want you to know that I am completely against you being here and think you should leave," he said.

"You know I can't do that," Inspector Gong said.

"I simply wanted to make my position clear," he said.

"Your devotion to your lady is admirable," Inspector Gong replied. The two stared at each other for a moment. Inspector Gong could not tell how old the eunuch was, they didn't age like real men, and his perfect skin and shiny bald head didn't help. His voice was clear, but slightly too high pitched. His lips were plump, which were exaggerated by the way he was pouting now. His large eyes were rimmed with thick, dark lashes any woman would envy.

"Follow me," Eunuch Bai finally said. He led the inspector down a hallway to another room where Lady Li was seated, waiting for him. She did not rise at his entrance. Her head was downcast and her hands fidgeted with a handkerchief. Eunuch Bai motioned for Inspector Gong to sit in a nearby chair.

"You may go," she said to Eunuch Bai.

"But...my lady..." he sputtered.

"I'll be all right," she said. "The inspector and I need to talk."

Eunuch Bai huffed as he left the room. Inspector Gong assumed he wouldn't go far though, and would probably be listening, if not watching, from the other side of the wall.

"Forgive him," she said. "He is very protective of me."

"I don't consider loyalty a crime," the inspector said.

"What happened?" Lady Li asked. The superiority and

haughtiness she first displayed upon meeting the inspector had vanished. She had not looked up from her hands and still seemed on the verge of tears, but she was clearly doing her best to remain calm.

"Are you sure you want to hear it?" he asked.

She pulled her eyes from her hands and looked at him. "Yes, I need to know."

"She was murdered," he repeated.

"How is that possible?" she asked. "The Forbidden City is one of the most secure places in the world. Everyone is watched all the time. It simply isn't possible."

"That is why I was called in," he said. "This is a terrible crime, not just against Lady Yun and your family, but the throne itself. The emperor and empress could be in danger. This is why I must find out what happened."

"Then why are you here?" she asked. "Why aren't you in the Forbidden City talking to the eunuchs, the maids, the ladies-in-waiting?"

The inspector paused. He didn't want to tell her he was incapable of conducting the investigation, that he most likely wouldn't find the killer since he couldn't interview the people most central to Suyi's life, but that was the truth. If he lied to her, he would be setting a terrible precedent for the rest of their conversation.

"You can't," she said, interrupting his attempt to come up with a good explanation. "That is why you are here. You can't enter the Inner Court. You are hoping this was a crime against Suyi and not the throne. You are hoping to find the answer on the outside."

She was clever, he had to admit. "Is it possible that someone outside the Forbidden City, someone from her family, a rival, a spurned lover, someone outside the walls would have wanted her dead?" he asked leaning forward and putting his elbows on his knees.

"No," Lady Li said. "She was just a girl. A child. I can't imagine anyone wanting to hurt her."

"But someone did," he said. "Someone not only wanted to hurt her, they hated her enough to kill her. There had to be something about her, someone in her life who hated her."

"Not that I know of," Lady Li said.

"Just start talking about her," he said. "Maybe something will come to you. Maybe something you don't realize is a clue. Tell me about her. I heard you were her guardian. Tell me about that."

Lady Li sighed and closed her eyes. "She was only a girl when I married her brother. But he and I had been betrothed for most of my life. Our families were close, so I knew her from the time she was born.

"Her mother was sickly and weak, always was. Her father died shortly after she was born. So she came to live with me after we married. She was such a sweet, funny little girl who loved to run and get dirty. She would chase the ducks around the yard and follow them into the pond, getting her clothes drenched and covered in algae. She was only eight or nine years younger than I was when I married, so she was like a little sister to me. But I was also Lady of the house, and her care fell to me, so she was like a daughter to me as well.

"I got with child within the first year, so she had to help me quite a bit. She became like a friend, and she was in the room with me, holding my hand, as my first daughter came into the world."

Lady Li began to sniff and she dabbed her handkerchief to her eyes.

Inspector Gong sat and waited for her to continue. He knew that she would eventually fill the silence.

"When my husband died, we mourned him together, sharing the funerary rites. He was the only man in her family. She did not get to mourn her own father, so she took the death of her brother hard, probably harder than I did." Lady Li gasped and put her hand to her mouth for a moment. "Forgive me, I should not have said that," she said.

"When she was fourteen, she followed in my footsteps and went to serve the empress, only a year ago. She was last home for Spring Festival. She was in such high spirits. Life in the Forbidden City is not easy, but there is always something going on, people to meet, things to do. She was happy and excited."

"Did she mention if she had made any enemies?" the inspector interrupted. "Another lady-in-waiting or a eunuch?"

Lady Li shook her head. "No. There are cliques and everyone is always vying for attention or favors, but that is just how things are. No one would ever go so far as to kill someone. Especially since there is no emperor to fight over."

"There is an emperor," Inspection Gong corrected.

"He is a child," Lady Li explained. "There are no wives or concubines. No scheming maids hoping to make the leap from servant to Lady. There is no clawing or grabbing for the love of a single man."

Inspector Gong nodded slowly in understanding.

"I'm sorry," Lady Li said. "I know none of this is helpful to you."

"It is," he said. "It helps me better understand what is going on inside the Inner Court."

"There are still some things you could do," she said.

"You could talk to the eunuchs. They know everything that is going on. Their trade is information."

"But would they betray their ladies?" he asked. "I doubt Eunuch Bai would ever speak ill of you."

Lady Li gave a small smile. "That could be a problem," she said. "Inside the Forbidden City, all of the eunuchs are the property of the throne. But some do form alliances with various ladies and with each other. If a lady moves up the ranks, she usually rewards those who helped her. So it is in the interested of the maids and eunuchs to help their ladies advance."

Inspector Gong thought about this, but decided to worry about it later. "Tell me more about Lady Yun's mother and father. Was her father's death suspicious in any way?"

"I don't know," she said. "I was a girl when he died. It was many years before my marriage, and my husband didn't talk about it. I'm not very close with his mother either."

"Maybe I should talk to her," he said.

"She won't speak with you," Lady Li said. "She is very traditional. She won't speak with a man. Besides, with her illness, she rarely leaves her quarters, so it wouldn't be appropriate."

"It's my job, Widow Li," he said. "I must speak to everyone."

"Lady Li," she corrected.

"What?" he asked.

"Lady Li, if you don't mind."

"You don't take the title widow? In respect to your husband?" he asked.

"In my girlhood, my hair pinning days, my wifehood, and my widowhood, I am still the same person. I am Lady Li."

Inspector Gong nodded his acquiescence. "Lady Li," he

said. "Well, I suppose I should go and alert your mother-in-law of my need to call on her. What is her name?" He stood to leave.

Lady Li stood as well, but shook her head. "She won't speak to you. And, I assure you, to press your case would be unwise."

"What am I to do?" he asked. "Do you want her killer found?" It seemed every avenue he wanted to take in this investigation was being blocked to him. He immediately regretted the question as Lady Li flinched from his verbal barb.

"More than anything," she said. "But pushing your way into my mother-in-law's bedroom will not get you the results you want. You are Han, you might not understand our ways."

Inspector Gong could not help but let out a small breath of surprise. How did she know he was Han? The Manchu had conquered China hundreds of years before, but had imposed many of their ways on the Han people and had adopted many Han ways in return. While the Han and Manchu liked to still believe they were separate peoples, in many ways, they were indistinguishable.

"How..." the inspector asked. "How did you know I was Han?"

"It is rather obvious," she said. "Your head is not shaved far back enough, your features are clearly southern, and your accent is...not quite right," she explained. "Does it ever get in the way of your investigations? Not being one of us?"

"No..." he said slowly. "At least, I didn't think so. Do you think other Manchu can tell by looking that I am Han?"

"I don't know," she said. "I only know that if my mother-in-law's neighbors suspected you of being indelicate with her, you might not leave the compound with your head."

"Would you speak to her?" he asked.

"Me?" Lady Li asked in surprise.

"Yes," he said. "I can tell you what I want you to ask and you could ask her for me. If you could just relay the information, it could help me. Provided you don't leave anything out."

"I...I don't know," she said.

"I think it is a brilliant idea," he said. "And because she is your mother-in-law, she will trust you."

Lady Li sighed and slowly agreed.

4

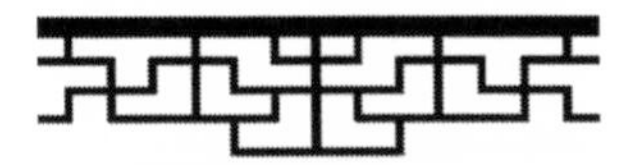

Lady Li tried to relax as two of her servants carried her in her sedan chair to her mother-in-law's house. Tension clawed at her shoulders and neck. She should have waited until the next day to call on her mother-in-law, but she was afraid someone else would tell her about Suyi's death first. The old woman had been ill as long as Lady Li had known her, and she was concerned that this blow would be the one to do her in. Lady Li thought about how shamefully she had reacted to the news of Suyi's death in front of the inspector. How would her mother-in-law react to the pain? She had no one left, no husband, no daughter, no son. Her household was small, only a servant, a cook, and a maid. How lonely she must be. Lady Li knew she should call on her more often, but she always seemed so tired. She worried about wearing her out, or used her exhaustion as an excuse not to call on her.

It was not very far to Lady Li's mother-in-law's house, only down a winding lane, but it would have been inappropriate for Lady Li to walk. A lady should never be seen in public. The sedan chair stopped just outside the gate of her mother-in-law's house, and she heard Eunuch Bai knock loudly. After several long moments, and several more loud knocks, the gate finally opened. She listened to Eunuch Bai banter with the servant for a moment before explaining why they were there. As expected, her mother-in-law's servant did not want to disturb her so late in the day, but, as rehearsed, Eunuch Bai insisted, explaining that if it had not been so urgent, they would not have come. Eunuch Bai then opened the flap to Lady Li's sedan chair and quickly ushered her inside the compound.

The home was quiet and felt dark. Even though the home was large enough for a family of many wives and children, none dwelled here. Most of the rooms went unused, so the doors were shut and candles and lanterns went unlit. Lady Li was led to the kitchen where she could sit by the fire and enjoy some tea with the old cook while the maid went to prepare her mother-in-law for her visit.

"It is so late in the day to be here, Lady Li," the old cook said as she poured the tea.

"I hope Popo will not be too angry with me," she replied, popo being the familiar term for mother-in-law.

The old woman swatted away the suggestion. "She doesn't have the energy to get angry," she said as she started chopping some green vegetables.

"Is her health worse than usual?" Lady Li asked as she slurped the hot tea to cool it as she drank.

"She doesn't push herself so much, so I don't know. She doesn't try to get out of bed or tend to her flowers anymore. But she's not dying, she's just weak. I don't know how to help her."

"What do the doctors say?" she asked.

"What do they know?" the cook asked. "They say her water qi is out of balance, so they try to fix it. Drink less water, drink more water, drink hot water, no spicy food, this is what they say, all different."

"What do you think?" Lady Li asked.

The cook stopped chopping and paused for a minute to think. "I think that when her baby was born, something else came out of her, leaving her weak. She was not like this before the baby."

"Do you mean Suyi?" Lady Li asked.

"Yes," the cook said, picking up her knife again. "But also with the little lord, your husband. That was the start."

Lady Li thought about this. There had been a large age gap between her husband and her sister-in-law, almost twenty years. If the birth of her son had weakened Popo to the point that she nearly died, it would explain why she would be reluctant to have another child.

"Did Lord Yun have any other wives or concubines?" Lady Li asked.

The old cook only shook her head.

"Why?" Lady Li asked. "He was wealthy and only had one son with his wife. If she couldn't have more children, why not get another woman?"

"Why do you ask all this?" the old cook asked. "Why are you here? I haven't seen you here for months and then you come, late in the day, asking all these questions. What are you up to?"

"Nothing," Lady Li said, returning to her teacup and smarting from the chastisement. She would have to be more discreet with her mother-in-law.

The old cook dumped the vegetables into a wok of oil, heated over a flame. The vegetables sizzled and released their fragrance. "Looking back does no good," she said.

Lady Li knew she was right, and the two sat in silence while they waited for Popo's maid to return.

Finally, she came back and led Lady Li to Popo's private sitting room, which was adjacent to her bedroom. Even though it was summer, there was a roaring fire in the middle of the room, and Popo sat near it wearing a padded chaogua over her chaopao. Lady Li was sweating as soon as she entered the room, but she did her best not to show her discomfort as she walked over and got down on her knees before her mother-in-law. "Thank you for seeing me, Popo," she said.

Popo reached out and took her daughter-in-law's hands. "It is nothing," she said. "I have nothing else to fill my days. Might as well answer when you take the time to call."

Lady Li stood and kissed her mother-in-law on the cheek before sitting down in a chair nearby, a small tea table between them.

"How are the children?" Popo asked as Lady Li poured tea.

"They are doing quite well," she replied. "First Daughter loves reading, and her calligraphy is beautiful. If she had been a son instead of a worthless girl, she might have been a great scholar."

"I told my husband not to ask your father for you. The women in your family were only good for giving girls."

Lady Li thought about this for a moment and realized that she was right. Her mother and her grandmother had only birthed girls. The only boys in her family came from secondary wives or concubines. "I cannot deny that I was a disappointment for you," she said. "If only I had given Lord Yun a son…" she wasn't sure how to finish her sentence, but Popo waved her hand to stop her so she didn't have to.

"What's done is done," Popo said. "You made him happy in other ways. Your daughters are good and you run your house well. If you had more time, maybe a son would have come. You were young and healthy."

"You are too kind to me, Popo," Lady Li said.

"Why are you here?" Popo finally asked her.

Lady Li took a steadying breath. "I need to talk to you about Suyi," she said.

"That girl," Popo groaned. "She never writes, she never comes to see me. What a daughter!"

"Life in the Forbidden City is not easy," Lady Li said. "She must work from dawn until the empress falls asleep late at night." Lady Li realized she was using the present tense and was doing a poor job of preparing Popo for what had happened.

"Filial piety is the most important quality in a child. The empress knows this," Popo explained to Lady Li, as if she were still a child.

"Popo," Lady Li said, reaching over and placing her warm hand on the old woman's cool one. "I have to tell you something about Suyi."

Popo looked at Lady Li with expectation in her eyes. Lady Li could see that she knew something was wrong. "Something happened to her..."

"What?" Popo asked.

"She...she's dead," Lady Li finally whispered.

Popo ripped her hand away as if Lady Li carried some vile disease. "What?" she finally asked. "How can you say such a thing?"

"I'm sorry, Popo," Lady Li said, her eyes filling with tears again. "I'm sorry. I...I just found out."

"Really? Is it true?" she asked.

"I believe it is so," Lady Li replied. "A man came from the Forbidden City and told me."

Popo lay her head back in the chair, closed her eyes, and

put her hand over her heart. Lady Li nearly fell from her chair as she kneeled beside her mother-in-law, gripping her other hand.

"Popo!" she said. "Please, Popo don't leave me. I need you!"

"What?" Popo asked, opening her eyes. "What do you mean?"

"I...I was worried about your heart," Lady Li replied.

Popo reached out and stroked Lady Li's cheek. "I was made for grief," she said. "Don't worry about me."

Lady Li wiped her tears away and sat back in the chair, but she didn't let go of Popo's hand. Lady Li was amazed at her mother-in-law's strength. She may be physically weak, but her soul was strong as iron. And her words held truth. The life of a woman was nothing but grief. Chinese women grieved that they weren't boys. Then they grieved when they were married and had to leave their families. They grieved if their husbands and mothers-in-law were cruel. They grieved when they gave birth to girls. They grieved when their daughters married and had to leave them. They grieved when their husbands died and they were left alone. The only happy part of a woman's life was when she birthed a son. Not having a son was a grief that Popo and Lady Li now shared. But Popo had a son, and now he was dead. That was a grief Lady Li had been spared, but she still knew Popo's pain.

The two sat in silence for a moment before Popo spoke again. "What happened?" she asked.

"I'm not sure," Lady Li replied. "They say that someone killed her."

"What?" Popo asked, sitting up straight, her eyes opening wide. "Why would someone do that? She was a good girl, wasn't she?"

"I believe she was," Lady Li confirmed. "She was a bit loud and excitable, but she would never hurt anyone, and she knew the importance of being chaste. I don't know why anyone would want to hurt her."

"Well, do the investigators have any leads?" Popo asked.

"They are trying to find out what happened," Lady Li said. "But...they need your help."

"My help?" Popo asked, surprised. "What can I do?"

"They think that maybe someone outside the Forbidden City might have wanted to hurt her."

"Oh, I can't believe that," Popo said. "She was just a girl on the outside of the walls. And I barely saw her. She lived with you. You are the one who would know."

Lady Li nodded. "Yes, but maybe someone wasn't after her specifically, but maybe they wanted to hurt the family."

"What do you mean?" Popo asked.

Lady Li paused for a moment before proceeding. It was such a strange thing for her to ask, something that smacked of disrespect, yet she had to ask. She knew the inspector expected it of her. "Did your husband have any enemies?" Lady Li finally asked. "I was never told why or how he died. Maybe his death had something to do with it."

Popo pulled away. "No, that can have nothing to do with it. It was so long ago."

"Popo," Lady Li said softly. "I know this is painful, but I have to ask. You must tell me. The empress herself wants to know what happened to Suyi. I have been ordered to ask you," she hedged.

Popo sighed. "I thought the past was dead and would be buried with me."

"If I don't think what happened has any relation to Suyi's death, then I won't tell anyone." Lady Li wasn't sure if she could keep that promise, but Popo seemed to take her at her word.

"I was married for four years before I finally became with child," she said. "So long, too long. But my husband couldn't afford a second wife, not then. So we tried and tried. Finally, I got with child. But the birth...the birth was bad. I nearly died, and the baby was weak. We feared he would not live to be a man. My husband insisted that we keep trying, keep trying for a healthy son. So we did, but no more babies came. Thankfully the baby, your husband, did grow strong.

"After my husband grew in rank, we became rich, so he bought a concubine, and then another. Still, no baby came. He bought a third concubine. Still no baby. For years he tried. He became obsessed with finding a woman who could carry his seed. The other girls, they never had a bad birth or lost a baby. They never got with a baby. He believed that all the women were weak and worthless. He never considered that he was to blame. He eventually sold them all away.

"I had not taken him to my bed for many years. I never recovered from the birth of my son. But he was desperate for more children. He couldn't bear the shame of having all these women but no children. He could hear the other men talk. Finally, I agreed to take him back to my bed. I was the only one who had given him a child, so maybe I could do it again.

"I did get with child again, and he was so happy. But when the baby was a girl, he was so angry. Then he was sad. He took a long scarf into his study and he never came out again."

Lady Li sat there in shock. Of course, she knew having children, mostly sons, was important to every man, but she had never heard of a man being so desperate, so despondent, for more children that he would kill himself.

"Did...did Suyi ever know this?" Lady Li finally managed to ask.

"I never told her," she said. "I never told a soul. Can you imagine the guilt she would feel if she ever knew her father killed himself because she wasn't a boy?"

"It wasn't her fault," Lady Li said.

"Of course not," Popo replied. "It was mine. I was the one who gave birth to her. I should have died after my son was born. Then maybe my husband would have learned to be happy with at least having him."

"Popo, please, it's no one's fault," Lady Li said. She could hardly comprehend what she was hearing.

"Anyway, you know how people talk. One of the servants found him. You know how they are. They never dared to speak of it in front of me, but I'm sure some people know. Your husband knew."

"He never told me," Lady Li said. She wondered if Popo's churlish cook was the servant who found him.

"Well, hopefully Suyi never knew," Popo said. "I told you it didn't have anything to do with her getting killed."

Lady Li nodded. "I think you are right. I'm sorry I made you tell me."

"I hope you do find out who did it, though," Popo said. "She was a good girl...my only one."

Lady Li felt a wave of guilt herself. She had not been a good daughter-in-law. She had ignored Popo, left her to wallow in sadness and loneliness. She had been grateful that Popo was not controlling and cruel like other mothers-in-law, too grateful. She had repaid her good fortune with her own cruelty. When was the last time she had sent her daughters to visit their grandmother? Was she really only concerned that they would tire her out? Or was she simply failing in filial duty? Without Suyi, Lady Li was the only one left to take care of Popo, so she resolved to do so.

"Popo," Lady Li said, "I want you to come live with me."

"No," Popo said quickly. "I'm fine right here."

"No, you're not," Lady Li said. "You are alone, and sick. You need to be with family."

"Family?" Popo asked. "I'm family now? Suddenly? After all this time? You worthless cow."

"I know," Lady Li said. "I have been a terrible daughter-in-law, and I would never ask your forgiveness. I only hope you let me spend the rest of my days repenting for my wicked actions toward you by bringing you into my home."

Popo shook her head. "I like it here. My belongings are all here, and your kids are too noisy."

"You can have the whole southeast wing to yourself. It's warm and quiet there. I'll make sure the girls learn to be quiet. But I think they would benefit from having their grandmother nearby."

"I can't leave the house," she said. "Who will make sure it is taken care of? I can't let it rot."

Lady Li had asked Popo to live with them before, but only out of duty, not because she wanted the old woman nearby. Usually, young brides did live with their in-laws, but Popo was different. She was so sickly, she knew that she could not be the head of the household. She would only be a burden to Lady Li, a baby in an old woman's body. In the past, Lady Li would offer for Popo to live with them because she had to, and Popo would refuse because she wanted to. Now, the situation was reversed. Lady Li wanted Popo to live with her, but Popo was refusing because it was polite. Lady Li had to ask Popo three times before Popo could accept, even though it was what they both wanted.

"Popo," Lady Li said, "I insist you come live with us."

Popo nodded. Her old eyes welled with tears and she did not speak for fear they would pour forth.

Lady Li patted Popo's hand and the left the room. She found Popo's maid. "Begin packing her things. You will all come into my household tomorrow." The maid nodded and went to see her lady for confirmation. Lady Li had no idea how her cook and Popo's old cook would work things out in the kitchen, but that was a fight for another day.

As Lady Li climbed back into her sedan chair, she lamented over the fact that she had not learned anything that would help her find out who killed Suyi.

5

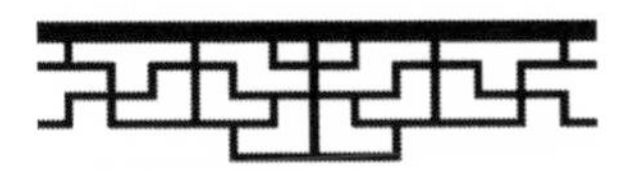

Inspector Gong had waited at Lady Li's home for her to return. He was sitting by the koi pond when two dark-haired girls came running through followed by a young woman. The girls stopped suddenly when they saw him and the woman quickly fled from sight. She clearly was not dressed for a male visitor. Her long hair was flowing free and she only wore a simple robe. The girls, however, bravely approached the stranger.

"Who are you?" the oldest one asked.

"I am called Inspector Gong," he said. "Who are you?"

"I am First Daughter," she said proudly. "And this is Second Daughter," she said motioning to the other girl who nervously chewed on the collar of her dress and stood slightly behind her sister.

"Nice to meet you both," he said. It was a fairly common practice to give children "milk names" that didn't hold much meaning. When they were older, children or their parents would usually decide on a name that better reflected the child's personality or was auspicious in some way.

"Why are you here?" First Daughter asked.

"You are very blunt," he said.

"I don't know what that means," she said.

"It means you say exactly what you think with no fear."

"I like that," she said, and both of the girls giggled.

"Who was that woman you were with?" he asked. "Was she your ayi?"

"No," she said. "She is Daddy's concubine."

"Ah," he said. "I heard your daddy was very rich."

"Yes," First Daughter said. "And when I marry, I will have a huge dowry. I will be able to marry any man I want. Even the emperor."

"Whoever you choose will be very lucky," he said. "What about your mother?"

"What about her?" First Daughter asked.

"What do you know of her?" he asked. "What do you think of your mama?"

"She's pretty," Second Daughter finally said.

"Yes, she is," he confirmed.

"She used to live in the Forbidden City, like Ayi Suyi does now."

"Do you miss Ayi Suyi?"

Both of the girls nodded.

"Did everyone like your auntie?" he asked.

The girls nodded again.

He wanted to ask them more questions, but he didn't want to give too much away. It would be up to their mother to tell them what had happened to Suyi.

"What's an inspector?" Second Daughter asked.

"It means..." How could he say he investigated crimes without letting them know why he was really there? "It is a sort of military rank."

"You're in the army?" Second Daughter asked, coming out of her shell.

"Not exactly, but I did have some military training."

"Can you teach me?" she asked.

"You want to join the military?" he asked.

She nodded. "I want to learn to fight with a sword and ride a horse and protect the empire like Mongeyisu, the Manchu heroine!"

"That is a very noble calling," he said.

"Teach me! Teach me!" she said as she started running around wildly.

"Okay, okay," he said. He walked to the koi pond and pulled out two reeds. He handed one to Second Daughter. "Here, hold this in your right hand. Hold it straight out in front of you. Now, swing left! Swing right! Hold it in front of you to block my attack. Here I come!"

The two of them chased each other around, swiping at one another with their reed swords while First Daughter laughed so hard she fell to the ground. This was the state of chaos her garden was in when Lady Li returned.

"What is going on here?" she demanded.

"Inspector Gong is teaching me to be a great warrior!" Second Daughter declared.

"Is he?" she asked, cocking one of her eyebrows at him. "Well, too bad he has to leave us before you can complete your training."

Both of the girls groaned in complaint.

"That is enough," Lady Li said. "Go find Madam Ling and get cleaned up before dinner. Both of you are like little pigs."

"Yes, Mama," they said as Second Daughter chased First Daughter across the garden and down one of the hallways.

When they were alone, Inspector Gong said, "Second Daughter has the makings of a warrior princess."

"Don't put such ideas in her head," Lady Li replied. "She is a lady, not a wild monkey."

"Come now," he said. "Manchu women were born on the steppes and rode and fought alongside men. Wouldn't you love to see your daughter bravely shooting an arrow from the back of a muscled steed across the plains as her foremothers did?"

"I don't need a Han to teach me about Manchu history," Lady Li replied curtly. "And I'd appreciate it if you would leave my family alone."

"You know I can't do that," he said, returning to seriousness. "I am under orders to find out what happened to Yun Suyi. I know you want me to find out what happened to her as well."

"We don't know anything," Lady Li said, exasperated. "You come here, bringing bad news and dragging up old, *painful* memories, all for what? Is it not enough that we have lost Suyi?"

"I take it your visit with your mother-in-law did not go well?" he asked.

"No," she said. "It did not. She has now lost both of her children. I have asked her to come and live with me. Hopefully my children and I can give her some comfort in her graying years."

"But you are sure nothing she told you could have anything to do with what happened to Suyi?"

"I am sure," she said.

"Do you need to tell me?" he asked. "Let me be the judge?"

Lady Li shook her head.

Inspector Gong decided not to push her. "Then there is

only one thing left to do," he said. "I have to get inside the Inner Court."

"As I said," Lady Li reminded him, "you won't get inside, and the eunuchs will only lie to you."

"I know," he said. "But you could get inside."

"What?" she asked.

"You could get inside. You served the empress once, you could volunteer to do so again. And you know how all the politics of court life work. You could get all the information for me."

She shook her head and waved him away. "You need to leave," she said. "I'm not going to discuss this with you."

"Lady Li..." he started, but she interrupted him.

"No," she said. "I am tired. I am sad. I am angry. I cannot even look at you right now. You need to go!"

Inspector Gong did not reply. She was right. It had been a long day for her, full of sorrow. He gave her a polite bow and then exited the courtyard. He did not even wait for Eunuch Bai to see him out. He mounted his horse and left without a glance back.

Lady Li's mansion, like many estates of the elite Manchu class, was located in the green, hilly area north of the Forbidden City, quite a distance from the Chinese—Han—City south of the Forbidden City. Like many of the Han Chinese of Peking, Inspector Gong lived among the endless hutongs that snaked around the Chinese City in an endless maze.

Inspector Gong rode back toward southern Peking slowly. He was in no rush, but needed to figure out his next move. This case was unlike anything he had investigated before. He had seen many murders, caught many criminals, but nothing inside the Forbidden City. The Forbidden City was exactly that—a city cut off from the rest of the world. It had its own rules, its own way of functioning. While he wasn't surprised a murder had taken place within the walls —he had learned that wherever people gather, crimes will take place—he was surprised that no one knew who did it and that they needed him, an outsider, to try and find out what happened. Justice often held a different meaning for the ruling Manchus.

Inspector Gong stopped by the Forbidden City and talked to the head guardsman on duty. He asked if there was any way in or out without the guards knowing.

"Of course there are," he said.

His blunt honesty surprised the inspector. "Why don't you close them off?" he asked.

"I don't know where they are," he said. "Only that they exist. I know that sometimes eunuchs and court officials slip in and out of the palace at night, but I have no idea how."

"That is unbelievable," the inspector said. "Isn't the empress worried about her safety?"

"Of course," the guard said. "But she has her own guards and her eunuchs are armed."

"Can the guards be bought?" he asked.

"Naturally," he said. "That is how most of the women sneak their lovers in at night."

"I can't believe what I'm hearing," Inspector Gong said. "The Forbidden City practically has an open door for anyone who wants to walk in or out."

The guard nodded. "I don't want it to sound quite that easy, or that I am shirking my duties," he said. "My men patrol the outer wall day and night, constantly. We use torches at night so we can see. If any of the guards are caught taking bribes to look the other way, they are executed. Getting in and out is difficult. But humans are like rats, they find ways to get where they want to go."

"What can you tell me about the girl's murder?" he asked. "Who found her? Where was she?"

"She was found her at first light, in one of the gardens. She had been killed sometime during the night. One of the ladies found her in the morning and reported it to a eunuch."

"I'll need to know which lady it was. I'll need to talk to her."

"I think her name was Lady Kwon, but you can't speak with her. She is one of the widows."

"Did she say anything about the scene? Did she describe it or say if there was anything unusual about it?"

"Not that I know of," the guard said. "She said she covered the girl's face with a white cloth and then went to find a guard. The guards took the body to the audience hall while the eunuch went to the empress. She sent for Prince Kung, and then he sent for you. That's all I know."

Inspector Gong sighed. His outside investigation was going nowhere. He had to get inside. He wondered if he should bribe one of the guards to let him in. It would probably work, but what would he do once he got inside? The Forbidden City was huge. He wouldn't know where to find the murder scene, and he wouldn't be able to talk to anyone. He needed help. He needed Lady Li. But how could he convince her?

He still needed to talk to Dr. Xue, who would be examining the body, but it was late and he was also tired. He decided to make his way home.

While his home was small compared to Lady Li's, it was nothing to spit on. It was one of the largest compounds in the southwest section. As he rode up to a gate, a male servant—not a eunuch—ran out to take the reins. The large wooden gate was opened for him automatically by another servant. Inside the compound, everything seemed alive. The family had already eaten dinner, so everyone was seated around the garden laughing, playing games, and talking loudly. Lanterns were hanging every few feet, giving the garden a warm glow. Several men—his father, uncles, and cousins—were playing mahjong around a square table. His mother, aunties, and sisters were sitting under an awning, fanning themselves in the warm night air. When his mother saw him, she stood and slowly walked his way. Her feet were bound, so she moved slowly and gracefully. When she reached him, she pulled him down to her and kissed him on the cheek.

"There is my beautiful son," she said. "Where have you been?"

"I had a busy day, Mama."

"You must be hungry," she said.

"Not really," he said. "Just tired."

"Nonsense," she decided. "All growing boys need to eat good meals."

"I'm not a boy, Mama," he said.

"Until you are married, you are a boy," she said as she led him to a table. "So unless you've hidden a wife under that chaopao, you're a boy."

She was right that he was old enough to be married, long past the age of marriage for most men, but he was in no hurry. Between his mother and his father's other wives and concubines, he had three brothers, two of whom were already married. He also had six sisters, but they didn't really matter. He was glad his brothers had been more eager to marry and start their own families. It took the pressure off of him and allowed him to live the carefree life of a bachelor he wanted. Well, as carefree as a man with such a stressful job could live. His services were constantly in need, and seemingly more often. China was undergoing many changes, and with change comes instability and crime. There were rebellions in the south and warlords to the west. The foreigners were constantly imposing their own rules and laws wherever they decided they wanted to live. The gangs in the poorer areas of the city were slowly encroaching on the more prosperous areas. And young people were always getting into trouble. While it was good that he had a constant stream of work, keeping him employed meant that someone else had suffered a great loss, and that could be hard to deal with day in and day out. Often, after finishing a case, he would unwind at a flower house with a bottle of *baijiu* on his lips and a whore on his lap. He would drink and enjoy the women until he passed out and couldn't remember the horrors of whatever he had seen and heard.

But drinking and whoring were far off in the distance tonight. He had to solve the case first. He didn't know how, but he didn't want to imagine what the empress would do to him if he failed.

The cook, an elderly woman from the countryside who didn't have bound feet, brought him a bowl of rice and several plates of food—fried fish, sliced potatoes, spicy pork. He took a few bites of each one, savoring the flavors. His mother sat down beside him.

"So, I heard your new case took you to court," she said.

He nodded. "I don't suppose I need to tell you why."

She shook her head. Word about the murder in the Forbidden City was already spreading. It would probably even be in the English newspapers by morning.

"What is the empress like?" she asked.

"She is how everyone says she is: a beautiful dragon. Watch out for her claws." They both laughed.

"What I wouldn't give to see inside the Forbidden City," she said.

"It is not so great," he said. "It is big, but cold. Nothing like this," he said motioning to the happy sounds from his large family.

"It is strange how the family with the largest house is also the smallest," she remarked. Indeed, it was strange. The Xianfeng Emperor had a dozen wives and concubines and was known to spend time with bound-foot Han whores. Yet he had only one daughter and one son. In all of the Forbidden City, the royal family was made up of the Dowager Empress, her stepdaughter, and her son, the little emperor. The Xianfeng's emperor's other ladies, and the widows of the emperors who came before him, all resided deep within the Forbidden City, but they were nearly forgotten, doomed to spend the rest of their days alone and childless.

"Money and power cannot always bring love and happiness," he mused.

His mother smiled. "I raised a scholar!" She laughed. "You say the word, little tiger, and I will find you a wife with big breasts!"

"Mama!" he said. "Don't say such things!"

"Why not? That is how you like them, yes?"

"I can't think about such things. I'm investigating an important case for the empress! I need to concentrate."

"Oh, of course," she said. "So tell me about this murder. Who was the girl?"

"I can't tell you anything, you know that."

"I can keep asking," she said. "Tell me, how can I help?"

"Actually," he said. "You can help me. The girl was murdered in the Inner Court, but I can't go there. I can't talk to the maids or the ladies-in-waiting. I can't even see where she was killed."

"Oh," his mother said, thoughtfully. "This is a problem."

"I need someone, a woman, to go inside and find information for me. Then she can report back."

"Do you need help finding a girl to do this work?" his mother asked.

"No," he said. "I already found one. She is related to the dead girl, and she used to be a lady-in-waiting to the empress. I thought she would want to help me, want to find the murderer of her kin. But when I ordered her to go, she refused!"

"You ordered her to go?" his mother asked.

"Yes, and she said no! Can you believe it?" he asked. He shook his head in disbelief.

Before he could react, his mother stood up and slapped him across the head. "You stupid boy!" she yelled.

He dropped his chopsticks and flinched from the pain. "Ow! Mama! What was that for?"

"What is wrong with you?" she asked as she sat back down. "Is this how you always treat women?"

"I don't know," he said. "I guess. Women are supposed to do as they are told."

"You are an idiot," she said. "Did I raise you? This woman is not your wife. She is not your whore. She is not a slave. You said she served at court. She is a Manchu lady! She doesn't answer to some piece of shit like you."

"I thought you loved me," he nearly whined.

"I don't like you much at all right now," she said. "And I doubt this woman, this lady, does either. So you went to this woman's house. Uninvited. Unannounced. You told her a young girl from her family had been butchered, and then you ordered her to go into the devil's mouth?" She swatted her hand at him as though he were a fly in her way. "Idiot boy."

"It didn't exactly happen like that," he said, though she wasn't very far off the mark. He did tell her that her sister-in-law had been murdered and then ordered her to deliver the news to her mother-in-law, which could not have been easy. He had completely left that part out of the version he had told his mother. He was certain his mother would never forgive him if she ever found that little bit out.

Lady Li barely had time to process what had happened and was probably scared, and yet he ordered her to drop everything and go to the very place her sister-in-law had been killed. She probably wanted to be with her children. She said she had loved Suyi like a daughter. Her death was a great pain and a great loss. She still had to plan the funeral.

He had been an ass.

"So what do I do now?" he asked.

His mother calmed down, placated by the fact that he was asking her advice. "Let her rest tonight. She will need the sleep to give her strength. Tomorrow, you go back and you *beg* her for her help."

"Yes, Mama," he said. "That is a good idea. I think I need a good night of sleep too." He kissed his mother on the cheek, waved to his family, and made his way to his own room where he stumbled into bed and was quickly snoring.

6

Lady Li could not wait for Inspector Gong to leave. He was insufferable. Cruel. He had no sympathy for what she had been through. She was still in shock and had completely lost her head in the situation, but after she returned home and saw him with her daughters, she woke as if from a fog. Her daughters! She had to protect them. She had already lost Suyi, she could not let something awful happen to them. She wanted to hold them tight and never let them go. She thought Suyi would be safe in the Forbidden City, under the ever-watchful eye of the empress. But she was wrong. If Suyi had not been safe at court, then nowhere was safe.

How dare that Inspector Gong force himself into her home, her world, and order her around. She should not have gone to see her mother-in-law, not then. Of course, she would have told her eventually, and she was glad she invited Popo to live with her, but it shouldn't have been then, not while she was still so emotional. Thank goodness Popo had been so strong.

As soon as Inspector Gong had left, Lady Li went to her room, shut the door, and hid her face in her pillows as she wept. She wept and wept as if she had never cried before. She had to get all the tears out because she didn't want her daughters to know what had happened. She had to protect them. She would tell them someday. They would miss their auntie. But not today, maybe not tomorrow either.

When she had finally cried out all she could, she sat up straight and called her maid to help her dress. Her maid redid her hair and helped her change her chaopao. She even added a few jewels to her hair and a long string of jade beads. When she went to dinner, she maintained her poise and instructed her daughters to sit up and hold their chopsticks correctly, as she did every evening. She acted as though nothing was wrong.

When Concubine Swan finally joined the meal, her eyes were heavy and she seemed drowsy. She picked at her rice and swayed back and forth as if she were listening to her own private musician. This was nothing new, but was becoming far too frequent. Lady Li knew Concubine Swan had been drowning her sorrows in opium, but she wasn't sure how she was getting it. She decided to ignore it for the time being. At least she wasn't sneaking out of the house to lounge in a dirty opium house.

"How are you, Concubine Swan?" Lady Li asked.

"I am well, my lady," she said in a soft and dreamy voice. "I saw the most handsome man today. Here! In our home. Can you believe it? Did you see him?"

"I know," Lady Li replied. "A most repulsive man."

"What I wouldn't give to feel the touch of a man like that...or any man..." her voice drifted off, so Lady Li decided to change the topic.

"Girls," she said. "I want to tell you that your grandmother will be coming to live with us."

"You mean Popo?" First Daughter asked.

"Yes, I mean Popo," Lady Li confirmed.

"Why?" asked Second Daughter.

"Because she is very lonely," Lady Li said. "And I think it would be good for you to have your grandmother close to you. There is much she can teach you."

"How? She never gets out of bed," First Daughter said as she shoveled rice into her mouth.

"Slow down when you eat," Lady Li said. "Your grandmother is very sick. You know that. But maybe we can find a better doctor for her. And she can still talk to you. She can tell you stories about the old days. Or about your father."

The girls didn't seem to respond to this. They didn't know their grandmother very well, but the house was large, so they wouldn't see her much anyway.

"When can we see Auntie Suyi again?" Second Daughter suddenly asked.

"Why are you asking that?" Lady Li asked, concerned.

"That man was asking about her," First Daughter said.

"Was he?" Lady Li asked. First Daughter nodded her head, but she didn't say anything else. Lady Li wasn't sure if she should press her. She didn't want the girls to ask about their aunt. She wasn't ready to tell them what happened. *Damn that man.*

"Will Auntie Suyi still be at the Forbidden City when I go there," First Daughter asked.

"I don't think so," Lady Li replied. "She will probably be married by then."

"Not if she's lucky," Concubine Swan piped up.

"That is enough," Lady Li said sharply. "Why don't you go to your room if you aren't going to eat, you wasteful cow."

Concubine Swan blinked slowly a couple of times before rising from the table and drifting back to her own quarters. Lady Li shook her head and motioned for one of the servants to follow her and make sure she got back to her own room safely.

"Was she acting like that when you were in her room earlier?" Lady Li asked.

"No," First Daughter said. "It was later, after the man left. I think she liked him, but she only saw him for a second before she left the courtyard."

"She is very lonely," Lady Li said.

"I hope when I get married, my husband doesn't die," First Daughter said.

"Marriage is a blessing and a curse, my little one," Lady Li said.

"Maybe I can just stay at the Forbidden City forever, like the empress. She gets to rule all of China and not have to worry about being lonely."

"It would be hard to be lonely when you are surrounded by so many smart and beautiful ladies," Lady Li said.

"Yeah," said Second Daughter. "We should just all live together, all girls, so we can keep each other company and not have to worry about a husband."

"Some women do that," Lady Li said. "In the silk communities in Canton. The women devote their life to art, to silk making, and to their embroidery work, and they never marry. They just live with each other."

"That sounds wonderful!" First Daughter said.

"Well, don't think you will be able to do that," Lady Li said as she waved a kitchen maid over to clear away their empty dishes. "You are both ladies of quality with big dowries. The men will be demanding the right to marry you."

"If I get to serve the empress in the Forbidden City," First Daughter explained, "the empress will choose my husband, if you don't pick one."

"That is very true," Lady Li said.

"Will she pick a husband for Auntie Suyi?" Second Daughter asked.

"I don't know," Lady Li said.

"Can we go to the Forbidden City and see her?" Second Daughter asked.

"No, she is much too busy to play with you."

"Well, when we serve the empress, she will have to play with us because she will see us every day!"

"You will probably be too old and too busy for playing by then," Lady Li said.

"No!" Second Daughter cried. "I'll never be old! I don't want to be a grownup."

"You better grow up!" Lady Li said. "I am not taking care of two babies for the rest of my life!"

The two girls got out of their chairs and started marching around the table chanting, "Never grow up! Never grow up!"

Lady Li hid her smile and laugh behind a napkin as the girls ran faster and faster around the table. Lady Li finally had enough, so she stood up and chased them around the courtyard. "You better grow up, you little creatures!" she said. The three of them laughed and screamed with joy as they ran up and down the long hallways of their large home. The maids and eunuchs also smiled and laughed as the mother and daughters ran past. It was not often the little family was able to lose themselves in joy.

Lady Li finally chased the girls into their bedroom and helped them change into older, simpler robes they used for sleeping. They all took turns brushing each other's hair.

Then, Lady Li got the girls into bed and told them the story of Mongeyisu, the historical Manchu bannerwoman. They had heard the story countless times, but they never tired of hearing it over and over again.

Finally, the girls laid down and started to sleep. Lady Li, though, couldn't leave them just yet. She wanted to sit and watch them, to make sure they were safe. Her mind wandered between staring calmly at the sleeping girls and her heart racing in terror at the horror inflicted upon Suyi. Even though Suyi had been living at the palace for some time, Lady Li never missed her more than she did right now. She started to realize that Suyi would never be coming home. She then realized that the empress had not sent her the body. She needed to be buried with all the proper funeral rites so she wouldn't become a hungry ghost.

Lady Li stood up and started pacing. What had happened to her that would keep her from being returned? Were they examining her? Poking and prodding her young body? Were they going to keep her? Did she need to pay for it? She would have to tell her girls what happened before she could bring the body home. They needed to be prepared. What if they dropped it off before she had time to tell them? She should have told them before they went to sleep.

She then thought about what her elder daughter said, about her going and serving at the Forbidden City. What if the killer wasn't caught, and he was still there when First Daughter entered the palace as a lady-in-waiting? Would she be in danger?

Lady Li realized that she needed more information. She needed to get Suyi's body back and she needed to make sure the killer was caught. That abominable Inspector Gong said he needed her help to solve the murder, and Lady Li realized he was right. He couldn't enter the Inner Court. She would have to do it. She wasn't going to offer to help him though. After the way he treated her so terribly, she wasn't going to approach him for anything. But if he came to her again and asked her for her help, she wouldn't say no.

7

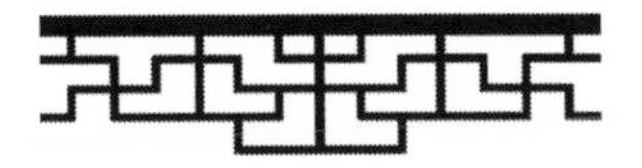

The next day, Inspector Gong took his time leaving his house and heading back to see Lady Li. Even though the murder of Suyi was important, the fact that he would have to apologize and beg Lady Li for her help did not inspire him to move quickly.

After he arrived at her home, he was met by Eunuch Bai, who only said "follow me" after opening the gate and "sit here" after leading him to a sitting room. The cook didn't say anything when she brought him some tea. He waited for over an hour for Lady Li to make her appearance. She probably had not expected him to return so soon, if ever.

Lady Li was worth the wait. She had taken her time in preparing to meet him this time, and she made sure her appearance met the highest standards for a Manchu lady. Her hair was pulled tight and smooth around a black batou headdress, which was decorated with fresh flowers and jade butterfly pins. She wore a long, bright red chaopao embroidered with dragonflies, bats, and the symbols for double happiness. It was edged in a deep midnight blue. Her pot-bottom shoes were tall and narrow. She wore three necklaces and several rings. Inspector Gong did not hide the fact that he was taking in her appearance from top to bottom and liked what he saw. Even though she barely showed any skin, Inspector Gong thought the way she dressed and carried herself was even more seductive than any brothel girl. He ran his hand over his mouth to hide a smile and scratched his wispy beard.

She was sending him a message. The fact that she took such great care in her appearance showed that she was going to forgive him. But the time he had to wait and the lack of hospitality by her servants clearly demonstrated her displeasure. She did not look directly at him, but averted her eyes. Her station did not require her to give him any of her time, even if he was there working under orders from the empress; he was not worthy of her gaze.

He stood and approached her. "My lady," he began. "I never expressed my sympathy for the loss of your kin. I am a worthless beast who should not even be in your lovely home. You are too kind to allow me within your gates again."

She inclined her head and bent her knees in the slightest bow, indicating her acceptance of his apology. She lifted her eyes and looked at him, causing his breath to catch in his throat. Her eyes, framed in the longest, darkest lashes he had ever seen, seemed to swim into his soul. But as quickly as she looked at him, she turned away. She took a couple of small, graceful steps back toward where he had been sitting. She motioned for him to return to his chair. After he was sitting, she slowly lowered herself into hers.

"Have you made any progress in your investigation, inspector?" she asked as she poured them two cups of tea.

"No, my lady," he said. "Well, unfortunately, I did find

out that there are ways into and out of the Forbidden City. Apparently it is common for the young women inside the palace to bribe the guards so they will allow their lovers in under the cover of night."

Lady Li paused for a moment at this. "Do you think Suyi was sneaking a lover into the Forbidden City?"

He shook his head. "I have no way of knowing if she did. My point was simply that her killer might not be a resident in the Forbidden City. The killer could have slipped in, did the deed, and then slipped out again before morning."

Lady Li shook her head. "I had no idea the Forbidden City was so easily accessible," she said. "Isn't this a security concern for the empress?"

"It should be," he said. "Do you know how common it is, for women to sneak men into the palace? Is this something every lady-in-waiting is aware of?"

"Not that I know of," she said. "I didn't know it when I served there, but I was very young and naïve."

"I wish I knew just how easy it was," he said. "There are many things going on behind those walls I wish I knew." He sipped at his tea. As he knew she would, Lady Li grasped his meaning.

"I have given more thought to your proposal," she said after a moment. "The one about me returning to the Forbidden City and looking for information myself."

"No," he said. "That was a foolish idea. I should not have asked such a thing. This is my job. I will figure it out."

"It is your job," she said. "But I think you would be able to find the killer much more quickly if you had access to the Inner Court, even if that information came from me, a lowly and untrained woman."

"I couldn't ask it," he said. "It could be dangerous."

"You didn't ask," she said. "I offered. And I know it could

be dangerous. Whatever happened led to my sister-in-law's death. What if something bad happens to another girl? I would never forgive myself if the killer is not caught and he is allowed to kill again."

He nodded. "I appreciate your assistance. I am sure that, together, we can find out what happened to Suyi."

At the mention of her name, Inspector Gong noticed Lady Li quickly sucked in a breath and her eyelashes fell on her cheeks. Her pain, her loss, was still very new and very sharp. He placed a hand on hers. Her hand was cold, as if there was no blood flowing to her fingertips. He had often noticed that grieving persons were cold. He wondered if the ghosts of the dead were sucking the qi from their loved ones, as if they were trying to hold on to this world and not pass on to the next.

"When will I receive Lady Yun's body?" Lady Li asked, not removing her hand from his warm touch, as she should have.

"It is being examined by a doctor," he said. "He will determine her exact cause of death and anything else of interest. When he is finished, I can have the body brought here if you wish."

"I do want her here," she said. "But I cannot have her arriving while I am away. I have not yet told my daughters what happened. But she must be buried before the forty-ninth day of her death."

"I am sure we can solve this crime by then," he said.

"I have made no arrangements for her," Lady Li said. "We have no burial plot planned. We never expected..."

That Lady Li had not made any arrangements for her sister-in-law's death was understandable. Not only did she not plan for the girl to die so young, she did not plan for her to die while living under her household. If Suyi had married, she would have joined her husband's family, even in the afterlife. It would have been their responsibility to provide a burial plot for her.

"After the doctor is done with his examination," Inspector Gong said, "I will have him keep her until you tell me what to do. I'll not bring her here or have her sent anywhere else until you tell me to."

"I need to tell Concubine Swan what happened. She will need to run the household in my absence." Lady Li stood, removing her hand from under Inspector Gong's. He stood as well. "I will go to the empress and offer to serve her this afternoon. How will I contact you with the information I learn?"

"I will figure that out," he said. "Please, set your house in order. I will return in a few hours."

She gave a small nod of her head and bent her knees slightly before exiting the room. Eunuch Bai entered and motioned for the door. Inspector Gong assumed that the eunuch had been listening to and watching their entire conversation.

"Tell me, Eunuch Bai," Inspector Gong began, "do you have any contacts at the Forbidden City that might be useful to our investigation?"

"I would not reveal them to you if I did," Eunuch Bai replied without hesitation.

"I did not think you would," Inspector Gong replied. "But your contacts could be of use to Lady Li. Would you be allowed to accompany her into the Forbidden City?"

The eunuch breathed out in frustration. "Most likely not," he said. "Eunuch selection at the Forbidden City is a very rigorous process. We cannot simply come and go. If the empress accepts Lady Li back, she will be assigned eunuchs and maids that have been approved for service in the Forbidden City."

"Did you serve in the Forbidden City before?" he asked. "Is that how you met Lady Li?" Eunuch Bai's silence was all the confirmation Inspector Gong needed. "Is it a common practice for ladies to take their eunuchs with them when they leave?"

"It happens, but I would not say it is common. Most people view us with derision. It is hard to form attachments with people who see you as less than human."

"But Lady Li was different?" he asked. "The two of you became close?"

"I will not discuss my lady with you," Eunuch Bai replied.

Eunuch Bai's protection of his lady was admirable and understandable, but her reliance on him, and that she would go to such lengths to keep him with her, was curious. It told the inspector something about Lady Li, he just wasn't sure what yet.

"Anyway, your contacts? Would they be willing to help your lady?" he asked. "Is there anyone on the inside that she can trust?"

Eunuch Bai opened the front gate. He gave a very small nod of ascent to the inspector's question. "I will give her, and *only* her, that information just before she leaves," he said.

The inspector nodded as he left. He headed for Prince Kung's mansion, which was not far from Lady Li's estate. Prince Kung's mansion was one of the most opulent private homes in Peking. The mansion had been an imperial residence for centuries, once belonging to a brother of the Jiaqing Emperor. Made up of countless living quarters and gardens, the mansion was practically a miniature Forbidden City.

The inspector was greeted by a eunuch at the gate who showed him into a sitting room near the front of the mansion to wait. He did not have to wait long for Prince Kung to appear. Prince Kung and Inspector Gong went back many years, though they had not always been close. For a long time, Inspector Gong was nothing more than the hundreds of other army men who were under Prince Kung's purview. But after the inspector proved himself to the prince by helping him solve several high-profile crimes around the city, the two men became friends.

"What brings you here?" Prince Kung asked, gripping his arm in greeting. "Tell me you have found out who murdered Lady Yun. The empress is beside herself with terror."

The inspector shook his head. "No such luck. I'm such a worthless dog, you won't believe what I have had to do."

"What is that?"

"I have had to enlist the help of a woman."

The prince laughed out loud and nearly fell into a nearby chair. "What? Who? Why?"

"The dead girl's sister-in-law, the Lady Li. I cannot gain access to the Inner Court. I need to know what is going on behind those doors."

The prince nodded and stroked his smooth chin. "The Lady Li, you say? She is no laughing matter. Smart, beautiful..."

"You know the lady?" the inspector asked.

"Of course. She served the empress during our flight to Jehol. The empress wanted her to marry me so she could keep her close. We were both amiable to the match, but I was already married and her family would not settle for her being a second wife."

"She is free now. Have you asked for her again?"

The prince waved the thought away. "I still have a wife and two concubines, I couldn't debase her by making her wife number four. She deserves better. Anyway, enough about the past. Why are you telling me this?"

"I will need to keep in contact with her and somehow keep her safe. Is there anything you can do to help us?"

"The Forbidden City is safe," he said. "I never would have thought a girl would be risking her life by going in there. Hell, I will send my own daughters there when they are old enough."

"But this is a different case," the inspector said. "We haven't ruled out why the girl was murdered. If it was personal, the killer might target Lady Li when she arrives."

"Would the killer be that brazen?" the prince asked.

"It is possible. From my understanding about where the body was found, in a garden, the killer made no attempt to hide what he had done. Even if the murder had been an accident, which I highly doubt, even in a state of panic killers usually try to hide their tracks. He didn't even move her to a more secluded area or put her in a pond to hide among the lily pads."

The prince considered this for a moment. "Does she realize the dangers she could be facing?" he asked.

"I think so," the inspector replied. "But she wants to know what happened. She wants justice for her family."

The prince nodded. "That makes sense, after her husband..." he trailed off.

The inspector wanted to press him for more information about Lady Li and her past, but he couldn't let the prince think he had any interest in Lady Li besides solving

Suyi's murder. "If things get dangerous," he said, "can she handle herself? She doesn't seem to be the type to give into hysterics, but can she remain calm and take care of herself?"

The prince tossed his head back in a muted laugh. "Oh, she is perfectly capable of taking care of herself. I remember during the empress's coup, she was so bold. She marched right up to Su Shun at one point and called him a stinking pile of pig dung!" He laughed again. He then looked at the inspector and cleared his throat to collect himself. "Never mind. Maybe you had to be there to see the humor in it."

The inspector sighed at that. How he wished he had been there, but he had been fighting Taiping rebels as a member of Xiang Army in the backwoods of Hunan at that time.

"Suffice to say," the prince went on, "that I think Lady Li is the best woman for the job. If there is a killer in the Forbidden City, Lady Li will root him out."

"But is there anything we can do to help her? Get messages to her or protect her?"

"I have some informants on the inside. I can have them keep an eye on her and report to me if anything seems amiss."

The inspector nodded. "Thank you. She is going there this afternoon."

"Thank you for letting me know," the prince said. "I'll head over there myself later and make sure she is all right."

"I'm sure there is no need to bother yourself..." the inspector said.

"Believe me," the prince said, "Lady Li is never a bother." The prince waved a eunuch over. "Be sure to see our guest out," he said before making a quick bow and excusing himself.

8

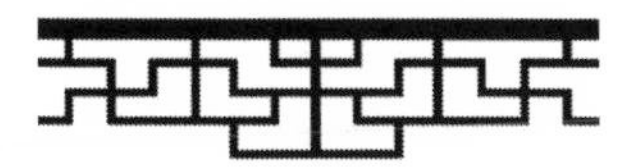

Lady Li's maid helped her dress in her finest chaopao while some of the other servants packed her traveling cases with clothes, jewels, her writing kit, her embroidery work, and other odds and ends. One thing Lady Li had learned while living at the Forbidden City previously was to always over pack. She had no idea how long she would be there, and life for ladies was terribly boring. It was also important to prepare for anything. When the court had fled from the Forbidden City in 1860, they packed everything they owned. The empress had over fifty mule carts filled with gowns, jewels, paintings, scrolls, embroidery works, porcelains, furniture, and anything she could remove from her apartments that was not nailed down. When they then had to flee the Summer Palace a few days later, the empress had no room left in her carts to rescue anything else. They watched hundreds of years of Chinese history go up in smoke from a nearby ridge after the foreigners sacked the palace.

Lady Li shook off the bad memories and sent for Concubine Swan. Concubine Swan seemed completely normal, not in a fog. She had suspected for days that something was wrong and was a little mad that Lady Li had kept her in the dark for so long.

"I cared for her too, you know," Concubine Swan said tartly. "And I thought you trusted me more than that."

"I do trust you," Lady Li said. "Which is why I am telling you now and leaving you in charge of the house. But I warn you, if I find out you were eating opium while my children were in your care, you will regret it."

Concubine Swan's eyes watered and she looked away. "You speak of your children and then you wonder why I eat opium?"

"No," Lady Li said. "I know exactly why you want to sleep and dream of a better life. That is why I haven't stopped you or punished you. But you can't do that while I'm gone. Do you understand?"

Concubine Swan nodded. "I am so ashamed."

"Don't be," Lady Li said. "Enjoy the next few days of freedom, pretending to be the lady of the manor and a mother."

"How can I be happy knowing what happened to Lady Yun? And knowing you might be in danger?"

"I'll be fine," Lady Li said taking Concubine Swan's hand. "I have lived in the palace before. And I will have people inside and outside to protect me."

"Why do you trust this inspector so much?" she asked. "You don't know him."

"He is known to the empress and to Prince Kung," Lady Li said. "And I trust them. That is enough for me."

Concubine Swan stood up to leave. "You better write to us every day. Let us know you are safe."

"I will," Lady Li said. "Popo will be arriving today. Greet her kindly and help her settle in."

Concubine Swan nodded and left the room just as Eunuch Bai entered. He spoke to her in a low voice. "When you arrive, you will be assigned a maid and a eunuch. If everything goes as planned, you should be assigned Eunuch Jinxi. You can trust him. He knows why you are coming and you can use him to smuggle letters in and out of the Forbidden City."

"I am impressed that you have been able to maintain relationships inside the walls after all these years," she said.

"Inside or outside of the city, we trade in information and connections, my lady," he said with a bow as he walked away to make sure her trunk was properly loaded into the sedan chair.

Lady Li met her daughters in the garden to tell them goodbye. "You must be good little ladies while I am gone," she said, giving them hugs. First Daughter tried to remain strong, but Second Daughter did not hide her tears. Lady Li did her best to fight them back herself. Since she had entered her husband's home, she had not left it for more than a few hours, and never overnight. She had never been separated from her children.

"I don't understand why you have to go," First Daughter said.

"The empress has sent for me," Lady Li lied. "I must go to her."

"But why?" First Daughter asked. "You already served her. Why do you need to go now? She already has Auntie."

"We are all servants of the throne," Lady Li said. "We must always do our duty and obey our empress and, one day, the emperor. Never forget, we are daughters of the eight Manchu Bannermen. When our empress calls us, we answer. One day, your time will also come."

First Daughter sighed and nodded her resignation.

Second Daughter continued to cry even though her mother hugged her tight. The little girl did not want to let her go, but she eventually let Lady Li hand her over to Concubine Swan.

As she was about to get into her sedan chair, Inspector Gong rode up. For a moment, her heart skipped a beat as she realized how handsome he was sitting astride his horse. She remembered the feeling of pride and warmth in the pit of her stomach when she watched her husband ride as well.

He jumped down from the horse and walked over to her, keeping his voice low as he spoke. "I have spoken to Prince Kung," he said. "He has contacts among the guards who will keep an eye on you, at least during the day."

She nodded. "Eunuch Bai has told me who I can trust on the inside. Once the empress has agreed to let me stay, I will send you a message."

"As soon as you can, you must find out where the...incident took place," he said, speaking carefully in case anyone had hearing keen enough to listen to their conversation. "Observe the scene as best you can and report everything back to me. *Everything*. Leave nothing out. Even the smallest detail could be a clue."

"Anything else?" she asked.

"Talk to the other ladies," he said. "But don't give yourself away. Be their friend and earn their confidence. Then, find out what they thought of her or what their suspicions are. They must at least have a theory about what happened."

"I can do that," she said, though her confidence was wavering. Her chin dropped to her chest as she suddenly felt nervous about her task and her hands began to shake. She didn't know how to be an investigator. How would she know what to look for? And what if people realized why she was there? What if the murderer suspected her just because she was Suyi's family? Would she be able to defend herself if she were attacked so brutally?

Inspector Gong must have sensed her apprehension. He took one of her small, trembling hands in his. Once again, Lady Li felt a surge of warmth when he touched her. "Do not be afraid," he said. She didn't respond; she wasn't sure she could. He reached up and lifted her chin so he could look into her eyes. "I believe you can do this."

She felt a sense of calm wash over her and regained her senses enough to realize that they should not be so familiar in public. Here on the street, anyone could be watching them. The gossiping tongues would certainly start wagging before her sedan chair even rounded the corner. She pulled her hand from him and responded with, "At least one of us does."

He chuckled. "Go, before you are late. I am sure the empress does not like to be kept waiting." He helped her into the sedan chair and finally released her hand as Eunuch Bai pulled the curtain over the opening and securely fastened it closed.

The sedan chair bearers hefted the chair up and Lady Li leaned back in her seat to get comfortable for the rocky ride to the palace.

Lady Li felt a jitteriness in her as she headed toward the Forbidden City. If only she were not going to investigate the murder, she would be looking forward to going back. She had many fond memories of her time there. It was also the first time she experienced freedom. She was no longer under the watchful eye of her mother and was able to do and say things she had never dared before. Lately, she had been feeling trapped again, bound by the rigid laws of society. Going to the Forbidden City seemed like a small escape once again.

Of course, it had been a turbulent and frightening time as well, but she persevered then as well. The empress had just given birth to her son not long before and was enjoying her new rank. She had only been a sixth-rank concubine before. The country was at war with itself and with outside forces. The Taiping rebels in the south were ravaging the countryside while the foreigners were battering the court. There were clashes in Peking and the coastal cities between local Chinese and the foreign interlopers. The emperor and Prince Kung were constantly at odds over how to deal with them. The emperor's health was not good, though, so the empress was secretly helping him read and respond to various letters and notices. But the empress was not very well educated herself, coming from a poor Manchu family.

At first, Lady Li had been jealous of the empress. They were near in age, but Lady Li was better educated, from a higher-ranking family, and, in her opinion, more beautiful. The only reason Lady Li had not been included in the emperor's consort selection process was because their birth charts didn't line up. He was a rabbit; she was a rooster. Such a match would have been rejected even if he had not been the emperor.

But over time, Lady Li learned just how difficult life in the palace was, that it was nothing to envy. The empress was extremely lonely. After she had become pregnant, the emperor was not allowed to bring her to his chambers anymore, so he found companionship among other women. After the birth and her recovery, he exalted her for giving birth to a son, but he never called her back to his chambers at night. She rarely saw her son. She was not allowed to nurse him, and his rearing and education were the charge of imperial tutors. She had few friends, and even fewer confidants. Her closest friend was her eunuch, Te-hai. Her days were strict and orderly and she had no privacy.

So Lady Li resolved the help the empress however she could. She befriended her and earned her confidence by helping the empress improve her reading and writing skills so she could better assist the emperor. Then, they all had to flee to Jehol. That was a terrifying and exhausting ordeal. They never knew if the foreigners were going to ride up behind them and drag them back to the city or if they would come across a band of rebels and be slaughtered on the road. They marched for weeks to reach Jehol, the site of a former hunting lodge in the far north. They arrived in the winter and the old building was freezing cold and had very few supplies...

As the sedan chair came to a halt outside the west gate of the Forbidden City, the Gate of Glorious Harmony, Lady Li chided herself for dwelling on bad memories. She needed to stay focused if she was going to find Lady Yun's killer, and she needed to be there for the empress.

One of her servants helped her out of the chair while the other began unloading her trunk. A palace eunuch greeted her at the gate and led her inside. The Forbidden City was every bit as awe-inspiring as she remembered. Every building was made of red bricks and tiled with gold. The beams holding the buildings together were red lacquered and painted with beautiful, colorful designs of auspicious animals or Buddhist scenes. The gardens were green and lush. Countless ladies—court ladies, officials' wives, princesses, former concubines—all walked around the palace grounds in the most beautiful gowns and the tallest hairdos. Eunuchs in their dark blue robes and red hats shuffled here and there in their silent linen shoes with their heads bowed.

Lady Li was led directly to the empress's palace, the Palace of Gathering Essence. When she walked through the two large front doors, she locked eyes with the empress immediately. The empress looked as though she wanted to run to her old friend, but, as always, she kept her emotions in check. Lady Li kneeled in the doorway. The empress dismissed all of her other attendants, even Eunuch Te-hai, and motioned for Lady Li to approach her. The empress stood, and Lady Li kneeled before her as far as she could go without actually getting on her knees and bowed her head.

"Long life to the Dowager Empress," Lady Li said.

The empress reached out and took Lady Li's hands in her own. Lady Li looked up and saw her eyes filled with tears. She stood, and the two embraced.

"I can hardly believe you are here," the empress said.

"Forgive me for not coming sooner," Lady Li replied.

The empress finally released Lady Li and motioned for her to sit near her. "I am sure these days have been difficult for you," the empress said.

"You are kind to consider me, my lady," Lady Li replied.

"It has been terrible here," the empress said. "I cannot sleep. I jump at every sound. I talk to no one. I'm nauseous. How can I trust anyone knowing there might be a...*a murderer*," she whispered, "in my midst?"

"I am sure you have nothing to fear," Lady Li said.

"How can you be sure?" she asked. "How could such a crime happen here, in my own home? I fear for my son. I fear for the rest of my ladies. They never go anywhere alone now."

"Staying together is wise," Lady Li said.

"Not only that, but now I am short a lady. Lady Yun was

such a comfort. She was so witty! And she knew just how I liked my gowns stored so they wouldn't wrinkle. Te-hai says he can just find a new lady, but how? Who? All of the young ladies I have sent for have made some sort of excuse. You wouldn't believe how many suddenly have ill mothers. They have all heard! They are all terrified to enter my service. It should be an honor for them no matter what has happened."

"You have me, Your Majesty," Lady Li replied.

"Oh, I couldn't," the empress replied. "You have already served. You have your own house to look after."

"I don't mind," Lady Li said. "At least for a little while, until the killer is caught. I hate to see you so distressed. Please, let me help you."

The empress paused for a moment. "You have no idea how I have missed you," she said. "I've never...I've never been able to trust in someone so completely since you left. None of the new ladies...they don't know. They weren't there."

Lady Li knew the empress was talking about their flight to Jehol and her return to Peking after her husband's death. It was a memory they didn't need words to recall.

"You have Prince Kung," Lady Li said. "He supported you when you took over as regent and he still serves you."

"It's not the same," she said. "He can't be here. We cannot speak privately."

"Are you sure?" Lady Li asked. "Is there no precedent for widowed consorts remarrying?"

"I'm lucky they didn't lock me in his tomb to die or at least leave me in a monastery," she said. "The idea that I would be anything other than a devoted widow is a completely horrid thought to them."

"There was Wu Zetian," Lady Li said, recalling the

woman who was once an imperial consort to Emperor Taizong. After his death, she was sent to a monastery to be a nun. After a short time, however, she seduced the next emperor, Emperor Gaozong, and became an imperial consort again. After the emperor fell ill, she effectively ruled in his name. After his death, though, she deposed her own son and appointed herself as empress and ruled for fifteen years. She was the only empress to rule in her own right in China's history.

"To speak her name in these walls is very nearly heresy," she said stifling a laugh. "No, I am doomed to be alone. I have accepted this," she said. "But that doesn't make it easy."

"Let me help ease your burden," Lady Li said. "Let me come back into your service, just for a short while."

The empress nodded and squeezed Lady Li's hand. "Welcome home," she said.

9

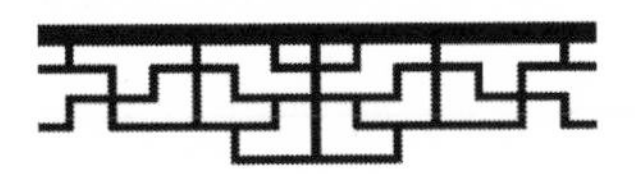

After Lady Li left her home, the Inspector finally found the time to visit Dr. Xue, who lived and worked in a hutong to the south of the Forbidden City.

The doctor's office was down a narrow alley, barely wide enough for two people to walk down side by side. Even though it hadn't rained in days, the alley was perpetually wet from lack of sunlight and the used water and night buckets that were continually dumped out of the houses that lined it. Inspector Gong stepped carefully to avoid mucking up his boots.

He entered the shop and was slapped in the face by a variety of smells. The heavy, musky scents of dried herbs and plants were not altogether unpleasant, but they quickly gave way to the smells of dried sea creatures, such as seahorses, sea cucumbers, and whole bins of dried fishes. As he stepped deep into the shop, closer to a door that led to a back room, the unmistakable scent of death began cloying at him.

Inspector Gong found it unbelievable that Dr. Xue had lived here for so many years. After the doctor had earned enough money to purchase a wife, she insisted they live elsewhere, but he couldn't afford to move them too far. He purchased the small house next door to his shop that was so close they shared a dividing wall.

Dr. Xue was advising a young woman on which teas she should drink to increase her fertility. There was no separate consultation room and the doctor didn't even lower his voice to try and protect the girl's privacy from whoever was listening. The young lady was apparently not yet married, but wanted to make sure she was ready to conceive as soon as she was. The doctor mixed a few different herbs and other items together and told her to drink it twice a day in the weeks leading up to her wedding day. The young lady thanked him profusely, handed him some coins, and shuffled out as quickly as she could on her bound feet.

"Will that potion actually work?" the inspector asked.

The doctor jutted out his chin. "Are you calling me a hack?"

"I just think that if you actually knew how to get women pregnant, you'd be a much richer man."

"Humph," the doctor replied. "She doesn't know if she needs help or not. She hasn't yet tried. She just wants reassurance. I actually gave her something to calm her nerves and help her sleep. After she is married a few months, if she doesn't get with a baby, then I'll try to figure out why and give her something to help."

The inspector nodded. "That is clever."

The doctor waved him away. "I'm not as feeble-minded as I look."

"Of course not," the inspector said.

"What of you?" he asked. "I'm surprised your mother has not come in for a medicine to give you to make you want a wife and children."

"If she does," the inspector replied, "don't give it to her."

"You are old, you are successful, and you like women, yes? You aren't one of those men who spends his evenings with opera singers, are you?"

The inspector sighed. "No, nothing like that."

"Then what's the problem?"

"I don't know. I think I would just find married life boring. I enjoy what I do. What woman could compete with that?"

"It's not about the woman," the old doctor said. "It's about doing your duty, being a filial son. Your job is to have many sons, elevate the family. You can still work outside the home, go do whatever it is you do every day, as long as you put sons in a wife at night."

"You speak wisdom, Dr. Xue," Inspector Gong replied. At this point, the inspector decided they had conversed enough that he could address the real reason he was there. "What about the woman I came to talk to you about?"

"That woman..." he said, shaking his head. "Big trouble. You must get her out of here before her spirit finds the body."

"What do you mean?" the inspector asked.

The doctor headed toward the door in the back of the room, the one that stank of death, and motioned for the inspector to follow him.

The backroom was lit by many lanterns, but it was still dark. The smell was horrendous. The inspector covered his mouth with his sleeve to keep from vomiting. There were several slabs spaced out in the room. Some had bodies lying on them, some were vacant. Several shelves against one wall were full of jars of body parts. The inspector could hear the squeaking of rodents coming from somewhere.

The doctor pulled back a sheet that was covering one of

the bodies. Inspector Gong hardly recognized the girl. Her skin was green and her cheeks were sunken in. Her mouth was slightly parted and her teeth were tinged black. He could see several small stab wounds in her chest that had suppurated and the doctor had cut her open and sewed her shut again so there was a long gash from her neck to her belly button.

"It is not such a bad job in the spring, autumn, and winter," the doctor explained. "But in these warm months, the bodies turn bad quickly."

"What can you tell me about her and her death?" the inspector asked, lowering his arm.

"She was young and healthy, but someone hated her," the doctor said. "She was killed by a woman, but a woman full of rage."

"What do you mean?" he asked. "How do you know that?"

"She was being poisoned by gu," he said.

"You must be joking," the inspector said, his mouth agape.

"I never joke about my work," the doctor said. "See the blackening of her teeth?" He pulled the cover down further and the Inspector noticed her belly was quite round. "She is swelling here. A sign of gu poison. And..." he picked up a knife and made a small cut to the inside of her arm. Black liquid oozed out. "Gu," the doctor said firmly.

"But why?" the inspector asked. "Surely there are easier poisons to get than gu. Where would a woman in the Forbidden City even find gu?"

"I have heard that the empress is fond of using poisons to get rid of people she doesn't like," the doctor said. "She can get her hands on anything."

"Yes, we have all heard the rumors," the inspector said.

After the death of the emperor, people whispered that the empress had a hand in his death. After she had the council executed and took the role of regent for herself and Prince Kung, some people were sure of it. The inspector had never put much faith in the rumors though. The emperor had been ill for years. After his humiliating defeat by the foreign powers and the burning of the Summer Palace, he simply couldn't return to the Forbidden City. From what the inspector knew about the emperor and from what Prince Kung had told him, the inspector assumed the emperor had died of shame.

"Do you sell gu here?" the inspector asked.

"Certainly not," the doctor said. "It's not just poison, it's black magic. Evil stuff."

"How is it made exactly?" the inspector asked.

"You take one of each of the poisonous animals—a scorpion, a toad, a snake, a centipede, a spider—and put them in a sealed jar. After many days, the jar is opened, and whichever animal is still alive is the most poisonous, but it is now more poisonous because it ingested the poison of the others. The victor is killed, dried, ground up. The black powder the animal becomes is the gu."

"But you said it was more than poison. You said it was evil."

The doctor nodded. "Such a death for the creatures is cruel. The poison is painful. You have to want the victim to suffer. It curses the victim. Causes a gu ghost, one who has to wander for eternity."

"It is also hard to come by," the inspector guessed.

"Indeed," the doctor agreed. "It is hard to make, hard to get, expensive. Only someone with extreme hate and the means could poison someone with gu."

"But she was also stabbed," the Inspector said.

"The girl was not given enough gu to kill her quickly. She was getting sick, suffering. But I do not know if this was intentional. Did the killer want the girl to suffer or did she simply not give her enough poison? I do not know."

"So maybe Suyi didn't die quickly enough, or she found out what was going on so the killer resorted to stabbing."

"That seems likely," the doctor said.

"You said she was killed by a woman. How are you so sure?"

"Women use poison, both to kill themselves and others. It is usually a clean death, no blood, no ugly corpse. But men can also use poison, or eunuchs, so how do I know it was a woman? Look at the stab wounds."

The inspector looked closely at the wounds in her chest. Again, he noticed they seemed small. He didn't notice their size before because there was so much blood. He had assumed the murder weapon had been a knife, but now he realized it had to have been a much smaller weapon.

"What do you think caused them?" he asked.

"Something small, narrow, and sharp," he said. He reached into a basket of tools near the body and pulled out something long and thin. "I found this among my wife's things," he said. "It fits these wounds almost perfectly.

The inspector took it and held it in his hand. A hairpin. Han and Manchu women wore elaborate hairstyles and decorated them with jewels, flowers, butterflies, and so on. One of the most common ways the hair ornaments were attached to the hair or the batou was with a long silver hairpin, about the length of a woman's hand. The inspector stuck the hairpin into one of Suyi's wounds and noted the downward trajectory.

"You are sure she was killed by a woman?" he asked.

"The killer was taller than she was. Could have been a eunuch."

"She wasn't wearing shoes when you brought her in," he said. "You know those ridiculous elevated shoes the Manchu women wear. There is no way to know how tall the killer was, if she was wearing shoes or not."

The inspector nodded. "So that means our killer could still be any woman inside the Forbidden City."

"My money is still on the empress," the doctor said.

"Be careful," the inspector said. "You could lose your head just for saying such a thing."

"Bah, who would come for an old man like me? But it is awfully strange. Her death was so violent, so painful. Small wounds take time to bleed out. Wouldn't she have been loud? Look at her hands. She fought back. She would have screamed. How could something like this happen without the empress knowing? How could it happen without her permission?"

The inspector didn't want to believe it, but it all made sense. He didn't know why the empress would want to kill her, but the empress was rumored to use poison, would have the means to get it, and could have ordered it done and easily covered up her own involvement. She could have ordered any other lady-in-waiting or maid to carry out the deed for her. The inspector then realized he had sent Lady Li to serve at the empress's side! What if the empress discovered why she was really there? She could be in danger!

"Ai-yo!" he gasped.

10

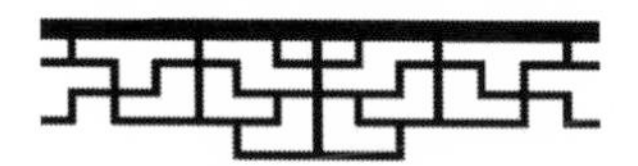

The empress's chief eunuch, An Te-hai, showed Lady Li to her quarters. During the reign of Emperor Qianlong the Magnificent, who ruled China during the 1700s, Lady Li's room would have been home to at least four imperial consorts. But now, with no proper emperor, only one empress, three widowed concubines who had also served the empress's husband, and a few aged widows still living decades after the deaths of their husbands, even a lady-in-waiting like Lady Li could have a palace to herself.

Lady Li's palace was basically one large room divided into smaller sections: a sleeping area, an office area, a sitting area where she could chat with guests, a large chair on a raised dais where she could receive messengers, and so forth.

When they arrived at her palace, a eunuch and a maid were waiting for her.

"I am Eunuch Jinxi," the young man said as he kneeled before her. He was quite young. Lady Li wondered how Eunuch Bai could know this boy well enough to trust him with her confidence. He could not have been serving at the palace when he was there. She was aware that without their manhood, eunuchs did not age as normal men and often looked young well into their later years, but this boy could not have been more than a teenager. She trusted Eunuch Bai with her life and wanted to trust his judgment in this, but she wasn't sure she could. Lady Li sighed but did not voice her concerns.

"I am Chu," the maid, also not yet twenty, said as she too kneeled.

"Has my position fallen so low that I am given only the most inexperienced servants?" Lady Li asked Te-hai.

Te-hai smiled as he inclined his head. "No, my lady. The empress has seen fit to only give you the smartest, quickest, and most beautiful of servants."

Eunuch Jinxi and Chu blushed at Te-hai's praise.

Lady Li had no idea if what Te-hai said was true or if he was only trying to compliment her, but she let a smile escape one side of her mouth, which put Eunuch Jinxi and Chu at ease.

"You're dismissed," she said to Te-hai.

He gave a quick, half-hearted bow before turning to leave. Lady Li remembered Te-hai from years ago. He had served the empress when she was nothing more than a sixth-rank concubine. No one else in the empire had benefited from the empress's rise more than him. Undoubtedly, the empress trusted him implicitly, and he was most likely utterly devoted to her, but was he abusing his position? He seemed very sure of himself and used to taking liberties. Even though he was the empress's confidant, she would have to keep an eye on him. But for now, she would have to figure out how much she could trust her own servants.

"Chu, may we have some tea?" she requested.

"Of course, my lady," Chu replied with a deep bow before quickly scurrying away.

This gave Lady Li a moment to evaluate Eunuch Jinxi alone. She said nothing, but watched him closely. The boy was calm and poised. After a moment, though, he glanced at her and looked her in the eye. It was only for a moment. Had Lady Li blinked, she might not have caught it. For a servant to look his mistress in the eye was considered a great insult, and she could have punished him severely for it, but she did not. She knew that his glance meant no offense, but was a message. In that brief second, she knew he was trying to put her mind at ease. He was trying to tell her that, yes, he had been sent by Eunuch Bai to help her, and she could trust him.

The boy had such expressive eyes. His whole face was quite lovely. It must have broken his mother's heart to have him cut, to know that her beautiful boy would never give her equally beautiful grandchildren.

Lady Li cleared her throat. "So, Eunuch Jinxi," she said, "what are we to do now?"

"Whatever you wish, my lady," he replied. "Perhaps you would like to send a letter to your family, let them know you have settled in."

And to Eunuch Bai and Inspector Gong, Lady Li thought. Perhaps this would be Eunuch Jinxi's first test of loyalty. Was he telling her that he was ready to be tested? Was he trying to earn her trust? Or was he trying to catch her? If she did write the letters, would he turn them over to someone else? Someone she didn't trust? *I'm getting paranoid*, Lady Li thought to herself.

"Perhaps you can answer some questions for me first," Lady Li said as she took a seat in the informal sitting area.

Eunuch Jinxi got down on his knees so she wouldn't

have to look up at him. “What does my lady wish to know?” he asked.

“You are aware that Lady Yun was my kin?” she asked.

“Yes, my lady,” he said. “My condolences for your loss.”

“Can you tell me which palace she lived in?” she asked.

“Yes, my lady,” he said. “She was housed in the servant quarters very near the empress’s palace. Her quarters were much meaner than yours, but the empress favored her very much and wanted her nearby.”

At this moment, Chu returned with a tea tray and placed it on the low table next to Lady Li. “Forgive me, my lady,” she said. “I wasn’t sure which tea you preferred, so I brought several: jasmine, pu’er, black. Forgive my stupidity and for not asking.”

“It is nothing,” Lady Li replied. “I am used to my own servants who have been with me for many years knowing what I like. I’ll take the jasmine for now.”

Chu nodded and placed the jasmine petals into a pot and then filled it with hot water. “Lady Yun also preferred jasmine tea,” the girl said.

“How do you know that?” Lady Li asked.

“I was her servant as well, my lady,” Chu replied as she poured the tea into a small cup.

There were endless levels of servitude and rank in the Forbidden City. Maids had maids who had maids, and almost everyone had someone they could order around. Even Chu would be able to bark orders at the kitchen maids when she requested the tea tray prepared.

“Is that why you were assigned to me?” Lady Li asked, sipping the tea.

“You’d have to ask Jinxi that,” she replied. “He requested I be assigned here.”

“Is that a fact?” Lady Li asked of no one in particular as

she eyed Jinxi. He didn't respond, but Lady Li was sure he was smiling to himself.

"Did you know her very well?" Lady Li asked Chu.

"Not as well as I would have liked," she said. "She was good to me, never beat me or yelled at me, but she was real careful about rules and boundaries. She didn't really confide in me the way some of the ladies do with their maids."

"Did she have friends among the other ladies?" Lady Li asked.

"I don't think so, my lady," she said. "She was favored by the empress, so I think the other ladies were jealous of her. The empress was probably the only person I would call her friend."

When Lady Li had served the empress years ago, she knew some of the other ladies were jealous of her. But no one had ever tried to murder her over it. There had to be a stronger motive than jealousy at play.

"So Lady Yun didn't have many friends, but did she have any enemies? Did anyone clearly dislike her?"

A giggle escaped Chu, which she quickly tried to stifle by putting her hands to her mouth. "Forgive me!" she said. "Oh, she had plenty of enemies. The empress was always favoring her with gifts, and she loved to show them off to the other girls and make their faces red. 'Crimson Flowers' was how she referred to the other ladies-in-waiting."

"Really?" Lady Li asked, her brow furrowing. She had never considered Suyi the hateful type. Had she known that Suyi was exhibiting such behavior she would have immediately put a stop to it.

"Oh, yes. And she was quite a sneak. She was always listening in on the other girls' conversations and paying the eunuchs for information."

"Did you know about this?" Lady Li asked Eunuch Jinxi.

"I did, my lady," he said. "I was going to tell you once you began to trust me."

"What about Chu? Can she be trusted?" Lady Li asked.

"I believe so," Jinxi replied. "That was why I requested her."

"Trust me with what?" Chu asked.

"Chu, I am trying to find out who killed Lady Yun," Lady Li said. Chu blanched. "Oh, don't worry, Chu," Lady Li said, placing a comforting hand on Chu's shoulder. "I am sure you are not in any danger. Yes, I am here to comfort and serve the empress during this time, but I must know what happened to my sister-in-law. I cannot allow her killer to go unpunished."

"Oh, my lady!" Chu gasped. "You shouldn't fret so! The empress has hired an investigator to find out who did it. You shouldn't worry about it. The killer will be caught."

"How?" Lady Li asked. "The killer is most likely here, in the Forbidden City, but the empress has forbidden the inspector from entering the Inner Court. I have probably learned more about Lady Yun's murder after talking to you for five minutes than he has discovered in the last two days!"

Chu started to cry and knocked her forehead to the ground. "I'm sorry, my lady. I didn't mean to upset you."

"Oh no, please don't do that," Lady Li said. "It doesn't help."

Chu did her best to reduce her crying to mere sniffles and wiped her tears away with the sleeves of her gown. "Forgive me," she mumbled.

"Just collect yourself," Lady Li said. She turned to Eunuch Jinxi. "Can you show me where Lady Yun was killed?"

"I can," he said. "But I don't know what good it will do. The area was thoroughly cleaned."

"I am sure," Lady Li replied. "But it might help me figure out...something. I don't know what, but Inspector Gong thinks that looking at the scene would be useful."

Eunuch Jinxi looked at a nearby clock. "I am sure it would, but the empress will be waking up from her nap now. She will most likely wish for your attention."

Lady Li sighed. "Oh, of course. I mustn't forget that I have another job to do as well."

"Don't worry, my lady," Eunuch Jinxi said. "We will find out what happened to Lady Yun."

Chu, with her red-rimmed eyes, did not look so confident.

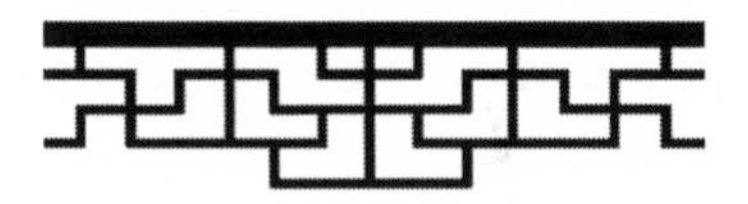

Lady Li was surprised at how quickly and easily she fell back into the routine of serving the empress. She helped the empress dress and freshen her hair and makeup as she rose from her nap. She served tea. She helped her practice calligraphy. They fed the empress's birds and walked in the garden. Lady Li didn't really take in any of it, though. The whole afternoon, all she could think about was Suyi and who could have killed her. The empress finally took note of Lady Li's absent-mindedness.

"You haven't heard a word I have said," the empress said as they were sitting alone after dinner.

"Every word you say is of the utmost importance," Lady Li replied.

"Then what have I been talking about?" she asked.

Lady Li made an educated guess. "Someone is causing you trouble."

"Always!" the empress said. "Someone always needs something from me. It never ends! I swear I have had the same headache for weeks."

"Being empress is a thankless job, Your Majesty."

"You haven't asked anything of me," the empress replied. "But your mind is not here. You were supposed to be here to comfort me in my time of distress, but you haven't given a single thought to me."

"Please, punish me if I have been derelict in my duties," Lady Li replied as she kneeled before the empress.

The empress scoffed and motioned for Lady Li to return to her seat. "Don't be ridiculous. I just want to know what has you so distracted."

"I wouldn't want to trouble you."

"I'm already troubled. Just tell me, then maybe you can focus on me again."

Lady Li sighed and considered what she wanted to say. She didn't want to reveal as much to the empress as she had to her new servants, partly to protect the empress but also to protect herself. If the empress knew that Lady Li was actually there to help find the killer, she was sure the empress would be angry.

"My heart is heavy with the loss of Lady Yun," Lady Li began. "I simply cannot imagine how such a thing could happen."

"It does you credit that you care so much for your

husband's family," the empress replied. "Of course, all of us become our husband's property and part of his father's household when we marry, but it is usually out of duty and tradition. You seem to have done so out of love for her loss to have affected you so strongly."

"She was just a girl when I married. How could I not love her?" Lady Li said.

"I heard you also took his mother into your home. You were quite lucky to not live under her thumb in the first place. But now, to willingly take her in? Lady Li, daughters will be forced to sing songs of your filial piety for generations to come."

Lady Li ignored the mocking tone in the empress's voice. "I only regret leaving her and my own daughters alone so soon after Lady Yun's death." The two women sat silently for a moment as the empress absorbed Lady Li's words. The empress rubbed her stomach a bit and sighed.

"Are you ill, my lady?" Lady Li asked.

The empress shook her head. "Just a bit of stomach discomfort. It has lingered for weeks but the doctors can find nothing wrong."

Lady Li had often wondered how the imperial doctors could ever diagnose and treat women in the Forbidden City. They were prohibited from looking at the emperor's women or even touching them. The doctor and patient would sit on opposite sides of a heavy curtain. The woman would put her hand through a slit, and the doctor would lay a thin white cloth over her wrist and feel her pulse for signs of imbalances. She then remembered Popo and how the doctors had not been able to treat her illness for decades. She must remember to find a better doctor for her when she returned home.

"Why are you here, Lady Li?" the empress asked, once

again interrupting Lady Li's wandering mind. "You have a perfect little world outside these walls. No husband to control you. Your mother-in-law is kindly toward you. You're wealthy. Why trade all that in to be back here, trapped within these walls?"

Lady Li decided at that moment that she was the worst detective in the empire, if not the world. If Inspector Gong knew what a mess she had made of things he would have her dragged back to her own home and never let her out. She had probably ruined his entire investigation. She decided it would be best to be at least partly honest with the empress.

"Actually I find being within these walls quite freeing," she said. "Before I served here as a girl, I had never left the walls of my family's compound. The few years I was here, we traveled to the Summer Palace and Jehol..."

"Fled to Jehol, you mean," the empress interrupted.

"Indeed, but it was quite exciting for me," Lady Li replied. "I met interesting men and women, even foreigners! I didn't have to practice my embroidery or read *The Analects* for hours. My mother wasn't controlling my every thought or move.

"I suppose I was wanting to experience some of that freedom again. Being a lady, a widow, a mother, it is not freeing. I have so much work, so many responsibilities and social constraints. I can only rarely leave my home or have visitors, and when I do I am constantly watched."

"I never thought about it that way," the empress said. "This place is a prison for me, as your own home is for you. I never thought that other women might find freedom here."

"You don't think the young women who serve here are

happy? Excited? Even liberated to be beyond the control of their families?"

"I suppose so," the empress said. "Life here is also regulated, but perhaps not as much as at their own homes. There is simply too much to do. The women can't be watched all day."

"Now that you think back on it, do you think Lady Yun was happy here?"

"Oh, yes," the empress said. "Certainly! She was always cheerful and helpful. I adored her company. She was such a bright spot in my otherwise boring life."

"Did you favor her?" Lady Li asked. "Give her special attention or privileges?"

"You mean, were the other girls jealous of her?"

Lady Li blushed at once again being so obtuse.

"I believe so. But that didn't stop me from doting on her, and it didn't stop her from basking in my attention. I only have the girls with me for a short time. Why shouldn't I keep the ones who make me happy close to me?"

"But could someone have been jealous enough to kill her?"

The empress shook her head. "I don't believe so. This is the imperial court. We are all ladies here. We don't go around stabbing each other when we get a little angry or jealous. It's all about favor and position. If someone hated that I was giving so much attention to Lady Yun, they simply would have worked harder to gain my favor, or have done something to cause her disgrace, something that would take her down a peg or have her sent home at the very worst. We are a civilized people."

Lady Li sighed and had to agree with the empress. Jealousy simply couldn't be a strong enough motive for murder.

11

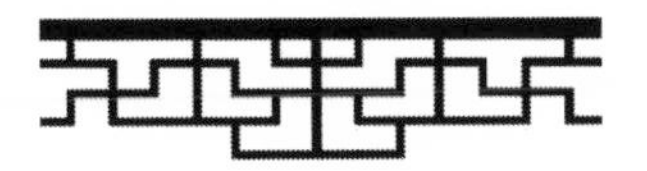

Inspector Gong rushed from Dr. Xue's to Lady Li's home. He had to find a way to contact her. Eunuch Bai would know how to reach her.

Inspector Gong banged on the gate to Lady Li's compound with more urgency than he intended, but he didn't stop. He banged on the gate until it opened and ran inside without noticing who opened it.

"I must get a message to Lady Li," he said.

"She sent a message for you earlier," a soft voice replied.

Inspector Gong quickly turned toward the voice and saw the concubine he had spied before. Her hair was down, only pulled back into a simple, loose ponytail that hung down her back. Her clothing was simple and her eyes were downcast. She turned and walked to a nearby table. She opened one of the drawers and pulled out a piece of paper. She handed it to him, all the while never making eye contact.

"Forgive me, umm...what is your name?"

"Concubine Swan," she replied with a small bow.

"Forgive me, Concubine Swan," he replied, taking the paper from her. "I hope I did not startle you."

"I should not have opened the door myself, but you were so insistent. I was afraid something was wrong. Is Lady Li all right?"

"Of course...I am sure she is. This is the first I will have heard from her," he said opening the letter.

"You must sit," she said, motioning to a nearby chair. "I will have tea brought."

"Thank you," he said.

A flustered Eunuch Bai rushed into the room. "Concubine Swan! You should not be dealing with this ruffian. Forgive me for being so slow. The young mistresses are looking for you."

"I will leave Inspector Gong to you then. I will send one of the maids with the tea." She gave another slight bow and turned to leave, moving as silently and gently as a ghost.

"Is she all right?" Inspector Gong asked as soon as she was out of earshot.

"It's none of your concern," Eunuch Bai snapped. "I see you got your message."

Inspector Gong looked it over before responding.

> *Inspector Gong. I have arrived in the palace and am situated in my quarters with two helpful servants. I have not yet learned much except that Lady Yun may have been causing trouble with the other ladies. I will speak with the empress this afternoon. Perhaps she can tell me more about the dynamics of the Inner Court. I will send more information when I can.*

Inspector Gong folded the letter up and began to pace. "Do you have a way to contact Lady Li?" he asked Eunuch Bai.

"I do," he said. "Not directly, of course. But I have ways of getting a message to her."

"I need to contact her," Inspector Gong said. "I fear she may be in danger."

"Of course she is in danger!" Eunuch Bai nearly shouted into Inspector Gong's face. "You sent a gentle rabbit into the lair of a vicious snake! You have no idea how conniving those women can be. Not to mention the eunuchs!"

Inspector Gong sighed. "It is a place of ball-less men and lonely women. Who would have imagined they could be so cruel to one another."

"What do you think would happen when you pit dozens of women against each other for the attention and affections of one man? They would all just live happily as sisters and willingly share?"

"But there is no man to compete for now," Inspector Gong pointed out. "The emperor is only a child."

"No," Eunuch Bai agreed. "Now they are all competing for the attention of the empress, who is much more discerning about who she favors."

"You lived in the palace for many years, correct?" Inspector Gong asked, even though he knew the answer. "Do you recall the empress being a particularly cruel woman? All those rumors about her poisoning her enemies and being unfaithful to the emperor, was there any truth to them?"

"I knew her before she was empress, back when she was only a concubine," Eunuch Bai explained. "When the emperor was alive, she was not a source of power. She knew her place. But when the opportunity to seize power came, she grasped it with a ferocity no one expected. That is how she and Prince Kung were able to stage the coup and overthrow the little emperor's regents so quickly and easily.

"So, in answer to your question, when she was a concubine, no, she was not cruel or power-hungry. She was faithful to her husband. But after she took the throne..." He paused. "There is no telling what she is capable of."

"Do you think she would harm Lady Li?"

Eunuch Bai furrowed his brow. "Never. They are good friends."

"Even if Lady Li was close to discovering that the empress had Lady Yun murdered?"

"How could you even suspect such a thing?" Eunuch Bai asked, his eyes widening in surprise. "You think the empress killed Suyi? What would lead you to such a conclusion?"

"I just came from Dr. Xue. He is certain the girl was killed by a woman. She was also being poisoned by gu, which is expensive and difficult to procure."

"This is preposterous," Eunuch Bai said. "What motive could she possibly have?"

"That is the only piece of the puzzle I am missing. And one Lady Li might discover."

"Ridiculous. The empress wouldn't kill one of her own ladies. If the empress is unhappy with a girl, she would just send her back home. If the girl committed a crime, as the head of the Inner Court, she could just have her executed without explanation. The empress has no need to commit murder. Besides, she asked you to find out who killed Lady Yun."

"She also prohibited me from conducting an effective investigation by barring me from the Inner Court. What if the girl knew something? Had found out some...secret? What if the empress couldn't send her away because she had information about something important but she couldn't execute her because she hadn't committed a crime?"

"You don't have any evidence for any of this," Eunuch Bai replied.

"Not yet," Inspector Gong said. "But who knows what Lady Li is discovering on the inside."

"What do you propose we do?" Eunuch Bai asked. "You can't go inside. You can send her a message, but that won't protect her. She can't leave so soon after arriving."

"Are you sure any message I send won't be intercepted by someone else? It will get directly to Lady Li?"

"I believe so. My lines of information are secure."

"We can at least warn her. Tell her not to look too closely at the empress. Don't arouse suspicion. And maybe she can find me a way in."

"Why do you need to go in?" Eunuch Bai asked.

"I am an inspector. I can see things other people can't. I need to see the crime scene."

Eunuch Bai sighed but didn't answer.

"One of the guards told me that it was possible to bribe your way into the Forbidden City under the cover of night. You wouldn't know anything about that, would you?"

"I suppose one could, theoretically. All people have a price...even you."

"Theoretically," Inspector Gong said. "*Hypothetically*, could you arrange such a thing?"

"That...is a lot to ask," Eunuch Bai hedged. "And would be frightfully expensive."

"You would put a price on your mistress's safety, Eunuch Bai?" Inspector Gong asked as he crossed his arms and did his best to hide a smile.

"Of course not," Eunuch Bai replied with a scoff. "It is just not something that would come together easily or quickly. And Lady Li would have to make arrangements on her end as well to make sure you aren't caught once you are inside."

"Well, get to it then," Inspector Gong said. "Start making arrangements to get me inside, and I will send her a message that she should expect me."

12

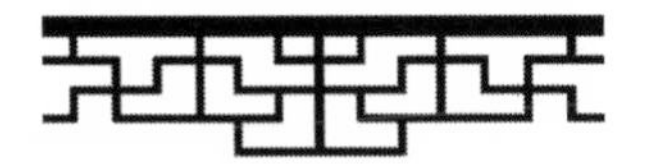

That evening, while the empress was playing with her son, Lady Li went to visit Lady Kwon. Lady Kwon was a former concubine of the late emperor, and she had been the one to find Suyi's body. Perhaps she knew something about Suyi's death that could help find the killer. Eunuch Jinxi and the maid Chu accompanied her.

As they approached Lady Kwon's palace, Eunuch Jinxi announced her arrival. Lady Kwon was standing in anticipation when Lady Li entered her sitting room. Lady Kwon stood straight as a pin and held herself with surety.

Lady Li bowed to Lady Kwon in deference to her station. Lady Kwon smiled in acknowledgment and motioned for Lady Li to join her on an embroidered couch.

"I was wondering how long it would take you to visit me," Lady Kwon began.

"Oh?" Lady Li asked.

"Of course. We are all just a little curious about Lady Yun's death, are we not? I am sure you want to know more about the particulars of her demise."

Lady Li was more than a little put off by Lady Kwon's

casual attitude about the matter. Death was not something to chat about lightly. To even mention death in the presence of the emperor or empress could mean treason. Han and Manchu peoples held many superstitions about death and treated them all with due caution. But Lady Li did not remark on any of this because Lady Kwon was correct, she wanted, she *needed*, to know more about what happened to Suyi, though not for the reasons Lady Kwon seemed to believe.

"I thank you for your consideration," Lady Li said. "I think knowing the particulars of what happened would help put my mind at ease, and it might help me better prepare her funeral rites."

Lady Kwon nodded knowingly. Chinese death rites were quite complex and designed to help the spirit of a departed person find peace. If the rites were not properly administered, the spirit would be restless and remain on the earth as a hungry ghost.

"Of course, I do not know how she died," Lady Kwon explained. "I only found her in the morning. I was walking in my garden, admiring the peonies, when I came across her."

"It must have been quite a shock," Lady Li said.

"Indeed, it was," Lady Kwon replied. "She was lying on her back. Her mouth was open as if in a silent scream. She was so pale she was nearly white. Her eyes...her eyes were wide, but staring blankly at nothing...I'm sorry, does this upset you?"

While Lady Li was upset by the description, the way Lady Kwon described the scene with such...*relish*, such passion, as if she were performing an opera, disconcerted her more.

"No," Lady Li lied. "Please, continue."

"She was filthy. Her face covered with dirt and her hair in disarray. Her gown was ripped and covered in dark splotches. I thought at the time it was dirt. Later I realized it was blood...so much blood. Her shoes were gone. Her feet were torn and bloodied, as though she had run over sharp stones with no shoes on.

"I believe her death was quite painful and that she was scared. She was running for her life."

Lady Li couldn't fight the tears. She turned away and covered her mouth to stifle the sobs. It was just too terrible. The poor girl. Running from her murderer, knowing she was going to die. Why didn't anyone help her?

"Oh, my dear Lady Li," Lady Kwon cooed, laying a hand on her shoulder. "Forgive me. I said too much."

"Why didn't anyone hear her?" Lady Li finally blurted out. "You said she died in your garden. She was running, terrified! How could you not hear her screams?"

"I don't know," Lady Kwon said. "I wish I had. I would have helped her if I could."

Lady Li took a few deep breaths to calm herself. There was something in Lady Kwon's voice that made her doubt she was telling the truth, or at least the whole truth. "Was there anything else of note?" she asked. "Did you see a weapon?"

Lady Kwon shook her head. "No. I don't even know what happened to her shoes. I suppose someone found them and disposed of them. Unfortunately, after I found her I immediately sent for the guards. They ordered us all to stay indoors for the rest of the day. I was unable to learn anything else."

"Do you know what direction she was coming from?"

"She seemed to have come from the west. She did leave some bloody footprints coming from that direction."

Lady Li nodded. She would try to find out where, or who, Suyi had been running from later. She decided it was best to change the topic before Lady Kwon began to wonder why she was asking so many questions.

"I am sorry to have forced you to relive that, Lady Kwon," Lady Li said. "It must be upsetting for you."

Lady Kwon frowned and paused before responding. "You don't remember me, do you?" she asked. "I was here, you know, a concubine for the emperor when you served here as a lady-in-waiting previously. Don't you remember?"

"Of course," Lady Li lied. There were so many ladies and concubines and former concubines within the walls of the Forbidden City, it was impossible to keep track of everyone.

"No, you don't," Lady Kwon replied. "You served the empress, and had no thought for anyone else."

"I was assigned to serve her. I had to give her my full..."

Lady Kwon held up her hand to interrupt her. "I'm not blaming you for anything, Lady Li, just making a point. Do you know what it means to live your whole life but not actually exist? Even when he was alive, the emperor barely took note of me. Did you know he was practically impotent? He could only be aroused by Han whores with their disgusting bound feet. How Concubine Yi conceived, I'll never know."

Lady Li stayed silent, both about the rumors of the emperor's impotence, which she knew to be true, and the fact that Lady Kwon was referring to the empress as Concubine Yi—one of her former, lower titles—instead of her proper title. Lady Li wondered just how lax the palace had become in enforcing the rules of decorum for a palace lady to speak in such a way, even in private.

"For the maids and the ladies-in-waiting," Lady Kwon went on, "there is still a possibility for life. They will eventually be married and go to their new homes. Most will have children. But for us royal consorts, us wives and concubines, our life is little more than waiting for death. We cannot marry, will never have children, and we can never leave. We are like ghosts. We no longer exist in the world.

"Concubine Yi escaped. By the good fortune of her womb she bore a son and became the Empress Dowager when the emperor died. She has purpose. She has a reason to wake up every day. We don't."

Lady Li sympathized with Lady Kwon. True, Lady Li was also a widow, but she had her daughters to raise and her household to run. She was also wealthy. But for the widowed consorts, they had nothing to live for. Their lives were similar to that of Concubine Swan's. No wonder Lady Kwon was so obsessed, so comfortable, with the idea of death. It was the only future she had to look forward to. The only thing that would end the monotony of day to day living.

"Why are you telling me all this?" Lady Li finally asked.

"I didn't kill your sister-in-law, Lady Li," Lady Kwon said, "but I can see how killing someone might be the only way to feel alive again."

"Are you afraid?" Lady Li asked. "Are you afraid of living in the palace with a murderer?"

Lady Kwon smiled, then let out a small snort of a giggle, then nearly bent over in a fit of laughter. "Fear death? Me? Why should I fear death? I welcome it."

To say that Lady Li was shaken when she left Lady Kwon's palace would be an understatement. But she did not pass up the opportunity to walk through Lady

Kwon's garden and see where Suyi had died. As they turned down a small path, Chu tugged lightly on her mistress's arm.

"Shouldn't we leave?" she pleaded. "That woman frightens me."

"I understand how you feel, Chu," Lady Li replied as she stepped over the row of stones surrounding the garden. "But I don't want to have to come back here. I just want to look around."

"Do you believe her?" Chu asked. "When she said she didn't kill Lady Yun?"

"I want to," Lady Li said. She looked at the ground, not sure what she was looking for, just for anything...unusual. "She said some frightening things, but I don't think she would have said them if she had killed her. She would have acted more innocent, don't you think?"

"I don't know anything about that. That sort of reasoning is beyond me. I think the killer would act guilty if she were guilty."

"If only life were that simple, Chu."

Lady Li gently moved some of the large flowers and leaves around so she could see under them. She lightly kicked at the dirt in some places. She finally came across an area where some smaller plants had been trampled down. The closer she looked at the area, a shape, like that of a human, seemed to take form. She began to visualize her dead sister-in-law the way Lady Kwon had described her, and it was as if she was looking at the body on the ground herself. She held her hand to her mouth and took a deep breath to calm herself.

"Is this where Lady Yun died you think, mistress?" Chu asked.

"I do, Chu," she said. "You can see here is where her

head was, and one of her arms fell here, and there are where her feet would have been."

Chu shook her head and looked away, obviously upset by the scene. "It's hard to believe no one heard anything. Look how close we are to one of Lady Kwon's windows."

Lady Li looked up and was indeed surprised to see they were only footsteps away from Lady Kwon's palace. Lady Kwon, or one of her maids or eunuchs, must have heard something. If they didn't, why? If they did, why did they ignore her?

"I don't think I trust that Lady Kwon," Chu said in a harsh whisper.

Lady Li hushed the maid. "We don't want anyone to hear you say such things." Lady Li kneeled down to get a better look at the ground where her sister-in-law died. She ran her hands over the dirt. Then, under a peony plant that was in full bloom, something caught her eye. She moved the plant aside and saw it more clearly—a gemstone. She picked it up and found it was actually a small string of blue gems, pearls, and carved silver ornaments. She stood up and showed it to Chu.

"It looks like an ornament from a hairpin, doesn't it?" Lady Li asked.

"Indeed, mistress," she confirmed. "Look, you can see the bit of link at the end where it would have originally been fastened to the stick."

"Lady Kwon said that Lady Yun's gown was ripped and bloodied. What if she had been stabbed to death with a hairpin?" Lady Li asked.

"You think this broke off in the attack?" Chu asked, her eyes wide.

"Seems like a possibility to me," Lady Li said.

"I don't know," Chu said. "Maybe it fell off of Lady Yun's

hair in the struggle. All the high-born ladies wear hairpins like that."

"That could be, Chu," Lady Li said. "But right now this is the only possible clue we have. Do you think it would be possible to find out who owned this hairpin?"

Chu took the gems and turned them over in her hand. "It's possible. All the ladies own these, but no two are the same. The Ministry of Domestic Affairs does their best to keep an inventory of the ladies' jewels, but it is not uncommon for the ladies to exchange their jewels as gifts or favors. It would be hard to track down."

"It might be hard, but we will have to try," Lady Li said as she took the jewels back and hid them in one of her sleeve pockets. She took one last look at the place where Suyi died. She then glanced back at Lady Kwon's palace and started when she saw a face looking back at her through the latticed window.

Lady Kwon slightly nodded her head at Lady Li. Lady Li gave a small bow in return. Then she took Chu by the arm and headed out of the garden. "We should go," she said.

"I agree," said Chu. "Between that creepy Lady Kwon and knowing Lady Yun died right here, I can practically feel the ghosts watching us."

They stepped out of the garden and walked back toward their own palace. Lady Li looked to the west and thought about finding out where Suyi had been running from.

"Oh no, my lady, not now," Chu implored. "After visiting Lady Kwon, then looking around the garden, if you go that way everyone will know what you're doing."

"You're right, Chu," Lady Li said. "We need to be more discreet. But tell me, what is west of here?"

"There are more gardens in the middle to separate the

east and west palaces, but the west palaces are home to more widow consorts."

"How many widow consorts are there?" Lady Li asked.

"More than I've cared to count," Chu replied. "You served when the emperor was alive, mistress. How many consorts did he have back then?"

"More than I ever cared to count, Chu," Lady Li replied. She thought about what Lady Kwon said about the consorts being invisible and realized she was right. Even when the emperor was alive, unless a lady was in the emperor's favor, no one paid them much mind. Now that the emperor was dead, they were completely inconsequential. What did they do with their time? Were they all as bitter and longing for death as Lady Kwon was? Was every widow consort in the palace a potential suspect?

13

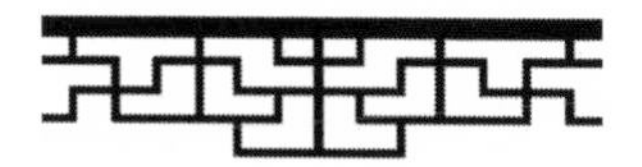

That night, long after everyone in the palace save a few guards should have been sleeping, Lady Li sat by a latticed window and waited. She had received a message just after dark from Inspector Gong saying that he would be coming to see her late that night. She wasn't sure how he would be getting in, but she was to wait by the west gate. Eunuch Jinxi had delivered the message, but he claimed he had not read it. She thought it best not to tell him. The less he knew about what was going on the better. She had dismissed Eunuch Jinxi and Chu for the night and told them not to return until morning.

Unable to rest until the appointed time, Lady Li decided to use the cover of darkness to do some more investigating. She wasn't sure why Inspector Gong was coming. She had told him everything she had learned in an earlier note. She didn't see a reason for him to risk entering the Forbidden City at night. Perhaps he didn't trust her judgment or thought the investigation was going too slowly. Or maybe he had learned something he couldn't tell her in a note. Whatever the reason, she hoped that some late-night snooping would reveal something of note she could tell him when he arrived. Maybe then he wouldn't think so little of her.

She didn't know why she cared what he thought. Such a boor. So rude and uncouth. A Han. He, his thoughts, and his opinions should mean nothing to her. Yet when she thought about him asking her for help, she couldn't help but feel something well up in her chest. He had treated her badly at first, that was true, but then he humbled himself and realized she had value. She was useful. He reminded her of her husband in that way. She had been valuable to him too, as more than just a wife and bearer of his children. He had been the one to insist she learn English. As a diplomat, he thought having a wife who spoke English could be useful to him. She was useful at first, able to visit with the British and American ladies in the Foreign Legation, but she spent so much of their marriage pregnant and nursing, and then he died so young, she did not get to help him as much as she wanted.

Then there was Prince Kung. He too found her useful and relied on her to help coordinate the empress's coup when he could not speak to the empress directly. The three of them had been quite a team.

She was lucky. She had found men who respected her and valued her for her brains and her wit. Few women, in any culture, were as fortunate as she. Yes, she needed to prove herself to Inspector Gong. She needed to feel useful again.

She slipped on a pair of Eunuch Jinxi's cotton slippers and waited until she saw one of the palace guards pass since he would not pass her quarters again for quite a while. She stepped outside and closed the door. She listened and looked into the dark for any sign that she was being watched. There was nothing. She did not take a lamp with her; that would be too conspicuous. She used only the light from the moon and from the few lanterns hanging outside the various palaces to guide her steps. She wasn't sure where she was going at first, where she should investigate at night. She decided to return to Lady Kwon's palace and go to the west to see what was there.

In her soft-soled shoes, she silently moved from shadow to shadow across the palace grounds and followed the path until it ended. *Strange*, she thought. *Didn't Chu say there were more palaces for the widows this way?* She peered through the darkness and let her eyes adjust to the dark. She realized the path no longer went west because there was a canal in front of her. Most likely the canal linked several ponds throughout the grounds. Across the canal there indeed were several palaces, but they could not be accessed this way. If she was running from this direction, it was not from the palaces. The path curved to the south, so Lady Li followed it.

But the southern path led only one place, back to the empress's palace. Lady Li froze as the palace loomed into view. Why would Lady Yun have been running away from the empress's palace? Did someone there...? Did the empress...? No, it was simply too preposterous for words. Just then, Lady Li saw something move closer to the palace. Lady Li ducked behind a bush and watched. The figure kept to the shadows as much as possible, as Lady Li had done, but he could no longer hide as he approached the main door. It was Te-hai. It was not abnormal for the empress's chief eunuch to be visiting her palace. Even at night, if she was working or distressed, she could send for him. But the palace was dark, save a few outside lanterns for security. If she had sent for him and needed him in an official capacity, why would he be sneaking around?

Once Te-hai slipped into the palace, Lady Li waited a moment to make sure he wasn't looking for followers, and then she also crept up to the palace. She didn't take the main path to the palace, but stayed within the shadows as she walked through a side garden. She went directly to the window of the empress's bedchamber and listened. She could hear hushed whispers, but couldn't make out any words. Then, the sounds changed. No longer words, but low gasps and moans. At first, Lady Li thought their conversation must simply be muffled because she couldn't possibly be hearing what she thought she was hearing. Eventually, though, as a married woman, she could not deny the unmistakable sounds of a woman being pleasured. But Te-hai was a eunuch. He couldn't possibly...

She had to know for sure. Maybe Te-hai had helped sneak a lover into the empress's palace before Lady Li saw him. Lady Li stood on her tiptoes and peered through the latticed window. There was a small fire burning in a brazier, just enough for her to clearly see Te-hai in the empress's bed leaning over her panting silhouette.

Lady Li turned away and crouched down, her hand over her mouth. Was it possible? But he had been cut...hadn't he? But then, a man's member wasn't necessary for a woman to be pleasured. Maybe he was just using his hand or...She bit her tongue to make her stop thinking about what was happening too deeply. She had to focus on what this meant. Did Suyi know? Did Suyi find out, much the way Lady Li just had? If it was discovered that the empress had a lover, even a eunuch, the lover would be killed. The empress would be shamed. The ministers would certainly petition to have her removed from power. She could even be put to death for betraying the dead emperor.

Did the empress catch Suyi peeping? If Suyi had discovered such a thing, it would be a secret worth killing over. Did the empress...? No! She couldn't have! If Suyi had displeased the empress in any way, the empress could have had her executed. She didn't need to murder her. She couldn't have. But could Te-hai?

Lady Li looked up at the moon and realized she needed to meet Inspector Gong soon. She had to tell him what she just discovered. Or did she? He would naturally jump to the worst conclusion and suspect the empress. If he dared to accuse the empress, she could have him killed. He wouldn't be that stupid, would he? Maybe. He seemed rather brash. But he needed to know. Maybe there was another explanation. Maybe he could help her find a solution.

As Lady Li made her way to the west gate, she thought back to when she was in the palace before. How long had this been going on? She had noticed that Te-hai seemed very sure of his place, of himself. Was it because he was her lover? She then thought about all the dozens of wives and concubines Emperor Xianfeng had, and all the emperors before. There was no way the emperors could satisfy, or even regularly visit, all their women. Was this something the eunuchs did? Did they pleasure the women to stamp down discontent in the Inner Court? It would be a way to meet the needs of the women without risking any children. But, no, that couldn't be possible. Most men didn't believe women had sexual longings or even received pleasure from sex. While it was common knowledge that men enjoyed sex and needed it regularly, women were only created to serve men and bear children. And if a woman did have sexual longings, it would mean she was not chaste. Chastity was the virtue every woman should strive to uphold. Of course, women knew differently. Lady Li knew differently. She had enjoyed making love to her husband. She had enjoyed stolen moments with Prince Kung...

So maybe the court did not specifically provide eunuchs to give women pleasure—that would not help the women remain chaste—but maybe this was an unspoken, yet common, practice. She did know that many palace women became attached to their eunuchs, even more than to their maids. And sometimes when a palace lady and her eunuch had a falling out, the two could be as wrathful as former lovers.

She thought about Eunuch Bai. She had never used him in such a way, had never even thought about it. But maybe he had entertained such ideas. He was devoted to her. She had even wondered if he loved her. Was he disappointed that she had never needed such intimacy from him?

Lady Li wondered if all the women, especially now that there was no emperor, had eunuch lovers. They were so lonely, so desperate. Why wouldn't they? It would give them some respite from their monotonous lives that were going nowhere. Perhaps Lady Kwon would benefit from...

What a cruel thing to think, Lady Li chastised herself. No woman should be so lonely that she would need the tender touch of a eunuch, a slave, to ease her burden. These poor women, reduced to such debasement. But what of Lady Li? Was her fate much different? She had not been widowed very long, only two years, and she had other aspects to her life, but she could not deny her own loneliness or the longing she felt late at night. What of Concubine Swan? She drowned herself in opium to escape her cruel fate. What of Popo? She had spent decades shut up in a single room. Such misery. What would become of Lady Li long after her daughters were gone and her money had been given as dowries? What would she live for then? Would she then also seek the solace of the touch of someone who was not even a man?

No, she could not let herself turn into one of these bitter women, one who only dreams of death. She had to find another path. She just wasn't sure how. For now, she needed to focus on the case; she had to find out what happened to Suyi. But afterward, something in her life had to change.

Finally, she saw him. She wasn't sure how he managed it, but Inspector Gong slipped through the west gate. Lady Li waved him over, and he joined her in the shadows.

14

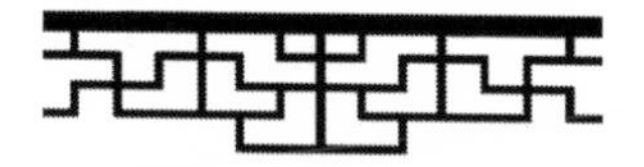

Not only had Eunuch Bai made the arrangements, he paid the necessary bribes as well. Inspector Gong had no idea how much the eunuch had paid, but after what he had learned about the penalties for such dereliction of duty, he knew it had to be a hefty sum. Inspector Gong had no doubt that Lady Li was wealthy, but it was surprising that her eunuch had access to so much of her money.

At the appointed time, Inspector Gong waited outside the west gate, far enough away the guard could not see him. Inspector Gong wasn't sure what would happen. Eunuch Bai had simply told him to go to the gate and wait; the way in would be made clear to him. Was he waiting for some sort of signal from the guard? Suddenly, the guard left his post, as if he was making nightly rounds. This had to be the signal, since a door guard would not leave his post to inspect the wall. After the guard was out of sight, Inspector Gong darted for the gate. To his surprise, the gate was unlocked. He couldn't believe how easy it was. Expensive, to be sure, but easy. He would have to talk to Prince Kung about strengthening the Forbidden City's defenses. This was no way to keep the emperor safe.

Once he was inside, again there were no guards present. He wasn't sure where to go, but then he saw something move, a hand waving at him from across the way. He ran over, as quietly as possible. He was so happy to see Lady Li he felt the urge to hug her. He didn't realize until that moment just how much he had worried about her safety.

"Why are you here?" she whispered.

Well, that was a fine welcome, he thought. "This place is dangerous," he said. "I needed to make sure you were all right."

"I told you in my notes I was fine. This is too risky. If you are caught..."

"Shh," he said. "Eunuch Bai arranged everything. The investigation is going too slowly. I need to see the murder scene. We need to find out who killed Lady Yun as soon as possible."

"Why the urgency? What happened?" she asked.

"The murderer is definitely in the city," he said. "Lady Yun was being poisoned."

"Poisoned?" Lady Li asked. "How do you know?"

"My friend, Dr. Xue, confirmed it. He said she was being poisoned by gu."

"Gu?" Lady Li asked. "How would someone in the Forbidden City even procure such a thing?"

"I can think of one woman who can get her claws on anything she wants," he said.

"You can't possibly think..." Lady Li paused. "You suspect the empress? Why? Why would she kill Lady Yun at all? What motive would she have?"

"I am still sorting that out," he said. "But she was killed

by a woman, viciously and painfully, and gu is rare and painful."

"How does he know?" she asked. "What were the signs or symptoms?"

"Her teeth were blackened, and when he cut her, her blood was black. While she was alive, she should have shown some signs of sickness," he explained. "But all the signs point to the empress even without motive. You have been here two days. Have you discovered any reason why the empress would be upset with Lady Yun?"

Lady Li did not reply. She bit her lower lip and looked away. She didn't want to talk, a sure sign that she knew something she didn't want to tell him.

"You know something," Inspector Gong said. "When were you going to tell me? Were you going to keep it a secret to protect your friend? Are you working against me?"

"Shh! Stop it!" she said.

Inspector Gong saw a light from the corner of his eye. He grabbed Lady Li and they huddled together. Neither of them breathed as the eunuch guards who patrolled the inside of the women's quarters of the Forbidden City walked past. He held Lady Li close to him. She was warm and soft. He let himself take a shallow breath and the scent of rose petals filled his nose. After the guards were long gone, he felt her squirm in his arms. He loosened his grip and stepped away.

"We cannot talk here," she said. "Follow me."

She led him past several gardens and buildings. He had no idea how she knew her way. This part of the Forbidden City was ornate, with many winding paths. It was completely different from the bare and utilitarian way the front of the Forbidden City was laid out.

They eventually came to a small palace. She opened the door and motioned for him to enter.

"We can speak freely here," she said. "I have dismissed my servants for the night."

"These are your quarters?" he asked. She nodded. He was surprised that she had dared to bring him to her private room. If they were caught, she would be ruined. But even if they had been caught outside the room, if it were known that she had smuggled him in, the consequences would be the same. For some reason he had not thought about how he was putting her in even more danger until just now.

"I am sorry I have put you in this situation, Lady Li," he said. "I never should have asked you to do this. The empress was right. I should have been able to do my job on my own."

Lady Li waved his apology away. "I need to know what happened. And I volunteered."

"So, are you going to tell me?" he asked.

Lady Li signed and lowered her head. "The empress... she is having an affair...with her eunuch, Te-hai."

Inspector Gong couldn't believe what he just heard. He sat down on a chair that was next to him and let the words sink in. "With...her eunuch? Are you sure? How do you know?"

"I saw them together," she said. "From outside. I peeked into her window when I saw him enter her palace tonight."

"And you are sure, even in the dark, you are certain about what you saw?"

She nodded. "There was no mistake. I mean, he is a eunuch, so I don't know exactly what they were doing. But he was in her bed, and they were acting as lovers."

"You realize this is a clear motive," he said, standing back up.

"In what way?" she asked.

"If Lady Yun caught them, the empress would certainly want the girl dead. That must be obvious to you."

"But we don't know that she caught them. Just because I know doesn't mean anyone else does. If she did catch them, that might explain a murder in the moment, out of fear or rage, but who was poisoning her? The empress wouldn't have killed her over a long period of time if she was carrying around a secret like that."

The inspector sat back down again. She was right. It didn't make any sense. "Maybe we are looking for two killers," he said. "Someone who was trying to poison her over a long period of time and someone who got angry enough to kill her quickly."

"That is possible," she said. "Apparently Lady Yun was the empress's favorite, and she was not very gracious about it. She liked that the other ladies were jealous of her."

"So anyone could have killed her," the inspector said. "You should leave this place. It is too dangerous. There could be multiple murderers running around."

"I don't think I can do that," she said. "The empress tasked you with finding the killer. If you don't, you'll be ruined."

"Why would you care about that?" he asked with a smile.

"I don't, not really," she said. "But if you don't find out the poisoner, the empress, and all the other ladies, will still be in danger. We can't stop looking, not just yet."

"But what will you do?" he asked. "What more can you do?"

"I am still following some leads myself," she said. "I visited the spot where Lady Yun was killed. I found a string of jewels, like the kind that would dangle from a hairpin. Lady Yun was stabbed, right? It could have been with a hairpin. It might have belonged to the killer. I am trying to find out who owned them."

Inspector Gong nodded, surprised at how quickly she determined the murder weapon with so little to go on. "According to Dr. Xue, the man who examined Lady Yun's body, she was most likely stabbed with a hairpin. It is amazing that you might have found part of the murder weapon. Will you really be able to find out who owned the jewels?"

"I am not sure," Lady Li replied. "I have to inquire at the Ministry of Household Affairs."

"What else?" the Inspector asked.

"I need to find out more about the empress and Te-hai," she said.

"No! No way," Inspector Gong said as he reached out and took her hand. "If she even starts to suspect you know something, she could kill you too. If she has done it once, she won't hesitate to do it again."

"I know how to be discrete," she said, not removing her hand from his.

"I would never forgive myself if something happened to you," he said. He felt her give his hand a small squeeze.

"I know," she said.

Did she? he wondered. Did she know just how much she had come to mean to him in so short a time? He had never met a woman like her before. She was resourceful and had the hidden strength of courage. The fact that she was beautiful was an exciting bonus. He could just imagine holding her body in his arms and kissing those soft lips.

"Is there anything else?" she asked. "Anything else I need to know or anything else you want me to do?"

He just shook his head, unable to speak. He just wanted her.

She nodded and walked over to the door. He stood, expecting her to open it and dismiss him. But, instead, she locked it.

She turned back to him and removed the pin from her hair. As she shook it out, he was amazed at just how long it was. It hung down the full length of her back.

"Would you like to stay?" she asked. "For just a little while?"

"More than anything," he managed to choke out.

She walked over to him, since he seemed unable to move, and loosened her sash. She opened her outer robe and revealed a thin inner shift. She stood right in front of him, her breasts nearly touching his chest. He reached up and touched her face. She wrapped her arms around him as she leaned up to kiss him.

Her lips were soft and sweet, just as he had fantasized. He kissed her harder, and she opened her mouth. His hands found their way inside her robe and he held her close.

He had never been with a woman before that he had not paid. He had never had what could be called a lover. But Lady Li, oh, she was exactly that. A proper lady. A sweet tasting, fragrant smelling lady. And she wanted him. *Wanted* him! She was not doing this out of duty or for coin. Was this normal? He had always been taught that women only slept with men to produce children or to earn a living. Did she derive pleasure from sex? Did the empress? Why else would the empress, or Lady Li, risk so much, risk everything, to take a man to bed?

He forced himself to pull away. "This is dangerous," he said. "We were just talking about the danger such a thing posed for the empress. It is the same for you. If we were caught..."

"Shh," she said. "I want this. It has been so long...so many years..."

"You are sure?" he asked.

She stepped back and removed her robe. She then undid the frog clasps of her shift at her neck and under her arm and let the thin silk fall away. She stood completely naked before him. He shuddered in anticipation. Her body was unlike any other woman's he had seen. It was so creamy white. Not a blemish, except for a few marks around her abdomen, reminders that she was a mother. The other women, the whores, their skin often looked sallow and dry, evidence of a hard life.

"In my home," she began, "I am alone. I am surrounded by children, servants, nosy neighbors. I could never bring a man to my bed without being caught and shamed. I know I am here to solve my sister-in-law's murder. I know this is a dangerous place. But this is the only chance I might ever have again to not feel lonely, to feel...a man..."

She turned and walked away. Inspector Gong followed. She led him to a separate bedchamber where a large kang stood covered with silk sheets and puffy pillows. The whole thing was ensconced in silk drapes. She sat on the bed and motioned for him to join her.

He quickly removed his clothes, hoping she was as impressed by his body as he was with hers. He kissed her as he pushed her back on the bed. She was supple and malleable in his arms and under his body. He took her quickly, far too quickly, he cursed to himself. But she was not done with him.

After they regained their strength, she laid him on his back and she rode him as though he was a mighty stallion. When he tried to grab her to change their positions, she pushed his hands away. She controlled the strength, the speed, the rhythm of their lovemaking, and it was glorious. He had no idea the varieties that one could enjoy in bed. Throughout the night, she showed him things he had never imagined. She was a far more skilled lover than he was, he had to admit, which surprised him since he had bedded many women in his days. But when a woman was working for coin, she typically wanted the act over as quickly as possible. He had not given much thought to what he had been missing out on. The dance, the prelude, the sensuality that surrounded sex was an incredible experience he was suddenly eager to learn more about.

As they laid in the darkness, many hours later, he held her and stroked her hair. For the first time, he entertained the idea of marriage. Men and women spent so much time apart, he had never imagined that a woman could be so interesting, so enjoyable. He thought a wife would be someone to live in his house, eat his food, and he would bed when he found the time. He never thought that a wife would be someone he could talk to, hold...love. No, he couldn't love this woman. Not yet, anyway. But he had to admit that having her as both a partner to talk to and as a lover was a life he could love. He was solving the most important crime of his career, and he had never been so happy.

15

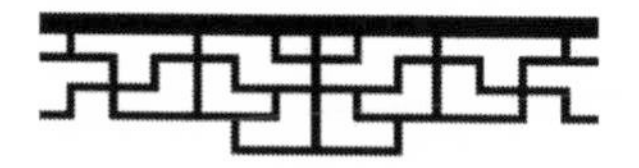

Lady Li felt completely content lying in Inspector Gong's arms, arms that were smooth and muscular thanks to his years in the army. His chest and stomach were similarly chiseled, and she enjoyed running her fingers over every inch of his body.

She was not sure what had come over her. She was so worried about becoming a bitter old maid and he was there. She saw a chance to take something for herself and she did not look back. She had no regrets. She would have her maid prepare some liangyang soup to prevent any unwanted consequences.

She had been a little concerned that he would not want to sleep with her. After all, the situation, investigating a murder, was not the ideal time to be giving into their carnal desires. And she was not the ideal bedmate for a young, strong man like him. She wasn't sure how old he was, but men were not considered old until they were into their graying years. They could marry and sire children until they died. She was a widow, a mother, considered old and used at only twenty-five. But when she offered herself to him, he did not hesitate, except to make sure it was what she really wanted to do. He seemed to have no qualms about her body. While they were making love, he seemed to worship her, taking and giving pleasure in equal measure. He was not as experienced as she had expected a man of his age to be, but he followed her gentle directions and she enjoyed teaching him, being in control a bit.

But all good things must come to an end, and he had to leave before they were caught.

"You should go," she finally said, but neither made a move to do so.

Inspector Gong ran his fingers up and down her arm as he stared silently at the canopy over her bed.

"You will need to leave before first light. The guards won't be able to turn a blind eye in the daytime."

He sighed. "I know. I just..." He didn't have to say it. Neither of them wanted this night to end. Was it for the same reasons? Soon, she would also have to leave the Forbidden City. Whether they found out who killed Suyi or not, she would have to return to her home. He would not be able to visit her there. Even if she did instruct Eunuch Bai to sneak him into her room after her daughters were asleep, what was the point? They could never be more than lovers. It was against the law for Han and Manchu to marry. Even if she did marry, her reputation would be tainted. If they somehow received permission to marry, Inspector Gong would then be in complete control of her money and property. No, they could not be together. Tonight was just...she just had needs that had not been met in many years. Taking a man to bed once in a while was one thing, but taking a lover or even considering marriage was not something she could do.

She sat up and pulled on her robe. “Do you know the way out?” she asked.

“Not exactly,” he said. “This place is like a maze.” He got up and put his clothes back on.

“What is next?” she asked as she dressed so she could show him the way out. “Where will your investigation take you?”

“I’m not sure,” he admitted. “We know the killer is here. We know the murder weapon is here. I am not sure what I can do on the outside to find out who killed Lady Yun.”

“Did the doctor say anything else? Anything that could help us track down the killer?”

He shook his head. “She was being slowly poisoned over time. But then someone killed her in a fit of rage, stabbing her with a hairpin. Just keep doing what you are doing. Find out who hated her enough to want her to suffer. Then find out who she enraged enough that they would kill her in the heat of the moment. My money is still on the empress though.”

“I’m going to prove you wrong on that point,” Lady Li said with a smile.

“For your sake, Lady Li, I hope you are right.”

She started to open the door, but he blocked her way as he leaned in to kiss her once more. She let him. Oh, how she would love for him to be in her bed again.

“Maybe,” he whispered between kisses, “when this is over...”

“No,” she said, pulling away and looking down. “We can’t talk about this.”

He nodded and opened the door. She led him back to where they had met, across from the west gate. He slipped to the door in the darkness and then he was gone.

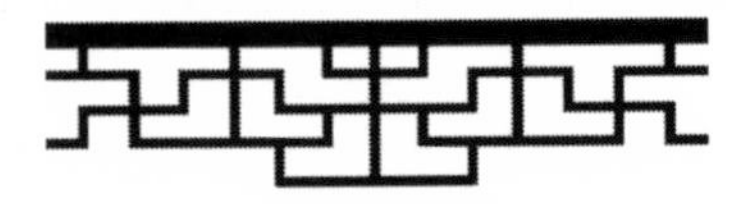

After the sun rose, Lady Li ordered Chu to prepare the liangyang soup. She only hoped the girl was too innocent to know what it was for. Lady Li then went to attend the empress. She wanted to talk to her about Te-hai. She didn't want to reveal exactly what she knew, that would be too dangerous, but she wanted to get a better idea of just how much power and prestige the empress had bestowed on him.

When she arrived, the other ladies-in-waiting were just putting the finishing touches on the empress's hair.

"Ah! Lady Li!" she exclaimed with a wide smile. "Please, come here. Go away, girls." She dismissed the other ladies, who scowled at Lady Li as they passed. "Can you fix this pin to my hair? You know just how I like it."

The empress held out a pin with a large jade butterfly on it. The empress loved butterflies. The robe she was wearing was embroidered with green and pink butterflies. From the butterfly on the pin, three long strands of pearls and gold beads dangled.

Lady Li took the pin in her hand and affixed it to the empress's batou so that the strands would hang just to the right side of her face.

"Oh, perfect!" the empress said as she preened in the mirror, turning her face this way and that. The empress was still quite young and retained many of her girlish mannerisms, at least in private. Those who knew her personally would find it hard to believe that someone so young had staged a coup, overthrowing China's most powerful ministers and becoming empress. Many people believed she was ruthless and cruel, and indeed she could be if the situation called for it. But here now, as she pursed her lips in the mirror and fussed over picking just the right necklace to wear, she seemed like any other young lady of means. One who should only be concerned with pretty clothes and giving orders to the maids who helped raise her children. Lady Li didn't want to believe that this woman, her friend, the woman she had helped put on the throne, would murder Suyi.

The empress finally seemed to be satisfied with her appearance and stood to leave, but then she wobbled a bit. Lady Li stepped forward, taking her hand.

"Are you all right, my lady?" she asked.

"It's nothing," the empress said. "Just a little dizzy spell from standing up too quickly. Come, I'm famished."

They went to the empress's private dining hall. The long table was laid out with over one hundred plates of food: savory meats simmered in sauces, sweet pastries, fruits from the southern province of Canton, and even chocolates sent over from foreign diplomats. The empress sat at the head of the table and a eunuch put a few selections on a plate in front of her.

"I'll take my leave for now, Your Majesty," Lady Li said. The empress would typically eat alone. No one was allowed to eat in the empress's presence, so it would be one of the few moments her maids and eunuchs had away from her demands, except those who served her food.

"Do stay," she said. "I'm so lonely. I simply hate having all this food here and no one to share it with. And I have just had no appetite at all lately. I'm hungry, but once I start to eat, I can barely stomach a bite. Please join me."

"Of course, Your Majesty," Lady Li said as she stood about halfway down the table.

"No," the empress said as she reached over and pushed a chair out. "Come here. Sit with me. Eat!"

Lady Li looked around the room. There was only one eunuch standing by, in case the empress called for anything, and he gave her a confused look. She walked up to the empress and sat precariously on the edge of the chair.

"Are you sure?" she asked. "It is most unusual."

"I know," the empress replied. "But I got so used to Lady Yun being here, I just can't stand to eat alone anymore."

"You would eat with Lady Yun?" Lady Li asked as she sat a little more comfortably in the chair and reached for a plum.

"Oh, yes. Here, you must try this duck in a sweet red sauce. I don't know what it is, but it is just marvelous."

"How did that come about?" Lady Li asked. "Lady Yun eating with you? That is quite out of the ordinary. I never ate with you when I was here before."

"You know, I'm not quite sure. We were just together so much, it just seemed natural for her to stay with me as we ate."

"No wonder the other women were jealous," Lady Li said.

"Were they?" the empress asked as she ladled sauce into a bowl for Lady Li. "I don't pay attention to such idle gossip. I have a country to run. I was a lowly court lady once. I know how those snakes are. I have to ignore it or it would consume every minute of the day."

"Do you also ignore the gossip about Te-hai?" she asked.

The empress froze and shot Lady Li a sharp look. She

stopped smiling and put the ladle back in its bowl. "What do you mean?" she asked cautiously. "What gossip?"

Lady Li took a small bite of the duck that the empress had served her and replied casually, "Just that he is rather sure of himself, of his place. He doesn't give the ladies and the ministers the respect he should."

"That's ridiculous," the empress replied, her smile returning, obviously relieved. "Te-hai is a perfect representative of court etiquette."

"Of course," Lady Li replied.

After they finished eating, they went to the empress's sitting room and chatted while they did some embroidery work. The other ladies-in-waiting joined them. There was Lady Song, the daughter of a court minister, Lady Deng, who was engaged to one of Prince Kung's younger brothers, and Lady Bao, the daughter of a diplomat who was currently serving in Japan. They all sat amongst themselves, chatting away, practically ignoring the empress even though she should have been the main object of their attention. Lady Li thought that if any of these young women had killed Lady Yun out of jealousy, she would now be vying for the empress's favor. But they all acted as if they couldn't care less about the empress.

Lady Li tried to engage the girls in conversation, but they would only give curt, one-word answers in reply. The longer they all sat together, the more irritated the empress became.

"You see?" the empress finally whispered to Lady Li. "You wonder why I am so bored and lonely? You see how they ignore me?"

It was odd, but Lady Li did not have an explanation or a solution. She was about to suggest they all take a walk in the garden together when the three girls began to giggle loudly. At this, the empress's head shot up, anger in her eyes. "Why don't you all just...ah!" She screamed as she looked back down at her hand. In her anger, the empress had managed to stab herself in the hand with an embroidery needle. Lady Li pulled out a handkerchief and rushed to the empress's side. She pressed the handkerchief to the wound. It was small, but it was bleeding enough for the empress to make a fuss. The other ladies also moved to her side and offered to help her. The empress's face softened as she basked in their attention.

"I think I will just go have a rest," she said. "Will one of you be a dear and have some calming tea sent to my bed chamber?"

"Yes, Your Majesty," the girls all replied in unison.

Lady Li removed her handkerchief and saw that the small puncture wound had already stopped bleeding. She waited until the empress and the other ladies had left before going over to a water basin to rinse the blood out of the cloth. When she opened the handkerchief to place it in the water, she gasped.

The empress's blood was black.

16

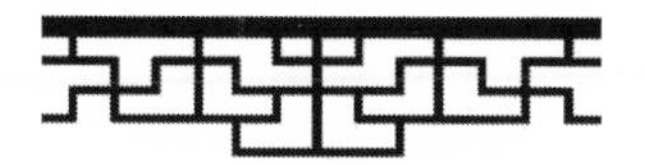

Inspector Gong felt like an idiot. He felt helpless. Lady Li was risking her life, putting herself on a collision course with a killer while he was trapped outside and he could do nothing about it.

Lady Li...In a way, she wasn't helping. She was a distraction. A beautiful, sexy distraction, but a distraction nonetheless. He had to get his mind off that woman and on the case. Maybe he was relying on her too much. If he didn't have Lady Li to help him, what would he do next?

Deep in one of the city's hutongs, down a dark alley so narrow barely a small cart could pass, was an old Buddhist temple. Buddhism was a foreign import, and still enjoyed only dubious success in the country. Unlike Daoism and Confucianism, schools of thought founded by Chinese scholars, Buddhism came from India. Even though small pockets of the religion had existed in China since ancient times, it grew exponentially during the reign of Empress Wu. A devout Buddhist, she patroned Buddhist monks and nuns and their temples. She gave the religion a legitimacy it had never seen before. Buddhism was once again seeing a resurgence of favor under the rule of the current empress, also a Buddhist. The temple Inspector Gong was seeking was one built during the reign of Empress Wu.

The alley leading to the temple was lined with shops for the dead, places where people could buy incense, paper money, paper houses, paper horses and livestock, and many other items that could be burned to accompany the dead to the afterlife. Other shops held the large gray memorial stones that would be carved with the names of the dead and the names of their family members and ancestors and placed in the family temple. There were also stalls for fortunetellers and matchmakers. Down one particular passageway, there were men and women who dealt in something much darker.

Some of the women in this area didn't even have stalls, they just sat on the street. There were some shops that were so dark, Inspector Gong wondered how anyone inside could see anything. If anyone wanted to buy a poison that bordered on the realm of black magic, it would be here. Unless the killer made it herself, but that wasn't a lead Inspector Gong could follow.

"I know what you are looking for," he heard a dry and cracked voice say.

He turned toward the voice and saw a little old woman, who was a hundred if she was a day, sitting on a low stool. "And how do you know that, laoma?" he asked, using the honorific yet familiar term for an older woman.

"Because it was only a matter of time. No one comes here looking for the most evil of poison who won't leave a trail to follow."

Inspector Gong crouched down next to the woman. "Can you tell me who it was?" he asked.

"Of course not, foolish boy," she said. "He did his best to

conceal his identity of course. But it was a man, a rich man, an important man."

"Can you tell me what he looked like?" he asked.

"Well, he dressed like a poor man that day, but I had seen him before, when he would accompany his wife to the temple. He would wear a dark blue chaofu with dragons embroidered on it."

Inspector Gong let out a breath. A chaofu—ceremonial gown—embroidered with dragons would only be worn by a court official. That meant that whoever bought the gu was a court minister, one of the empress's inner circle of advisors. But there were many of them. He had to narrow it down further.

"Do you remember anything else about his clothes? The insignia on the front of his chaofu?"

"It was a golden bird," she said.

A golden bird? It had to be the golden pheasant. The emblem of a second-class court official. A second-class official was a high-ranking person indeed, just below the court princes such as Prince Kung. There were only three, maybe four men who held such a title now.

He handed the woman a few coins as thanks for the information. "Anything else you can tell me, laoma?" he asked.

She shook her head. "Not about that man, but I can tell you that if you keep pursuing that woman, it will not end well."

Inspector Gong, usually adept at hiding his emotions when conducting an interview, felt his face drop and his heart stop. "What...what do you mean?" he asked.

"She is not one of us," she said, meaning Han. She was obviously Han since she had bound feet. "There is a reason they are separate from us. They think it is to keep themselves pure, but it is a protection for us from Heaven. They are just foreigners. Eventually, they will fall, and they will drag everyone they can down with them."

"Be careful, laoma," Inspector Gong said. "To speak so of the emperor in such a way, it is treason."

She waved him away and slowly stood, leaning on a crooked walking stick for support. "It is only truth," she said. "What I say is true, of the Manchu and that woman. Leave her alone, Gong Anguo."

"How do you know my name?" he asked.

The old woman waved him off. "Your mother, she is one of my best customers."

Inspector Gong rolled his eyes. No wonder the woman knew so much.

"She comes here every week, wanting to know when you will let her find you a daughter-in-law," the woman explained.

"And what do you tell her?" he asked.

"What she wants to hear," she said without a hint of remorse for lying to his mother and taking her money on a regular basis. "That you will settle down soon enough. She just needs to be patient."

"Thank you for calming her worries and keeping her off my back," he said as he turned to leave.

"But I could tell you the truth..." she said as she rubbed her fingers together.

He did not put much stock in fortune tellers, but he figured he owed her for the what she had done for his mother. So he handed her two coins.

"Give me your right palm, if you want to know the future," she said. He sighed and gave her his hand.

She held it to the light and hem and hawed for a moment.

"I cannot say for certain," she said. "But you are coming in a fork in the road. One path will lead to misery for yourself and happiness for others; the other path, to misery for others but happiness for yourself...eventually. It is a hard road."

"So disappoint myself or disappoint my family?" he asked. "Those are my only options in life?"

"It is not really a choice, is it?" she asked. "Family, duty, honor. These are the most important things in life. When the time comes, you will know which path to take."

Just then, a small group of people made their way down the alley. Inspector Gong stepped back to let them pass. When the crowd cleared, Inspector Gong looked again, and the old woman was gone.

17

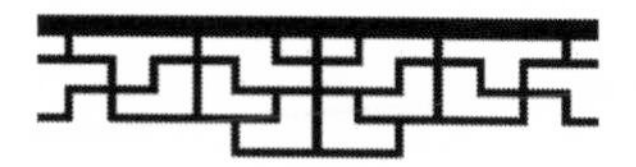

Lady Li retched into a bowl. She had eaten from the empress's table. That had to be where the poison was coming from. She said Lady Yun had eaten with her as well. That must be how Lady Yun was poisoned. The poison wasn't meant for Lady Yun. It was meant for the empress! But how? The empress's food was prepared by her own cooks, people who didn't prepare food for anyone else in the palace. And the food was tasted by several testers who all tried the food before it was sent to her table. But if the food only contained a small amount of poison, the testers, and the empress, wouldn't get sick immediately after trying it. It could take days or weeks for the poison to build up in her system enough to kill her. How long had this been going on? Had Suyi discovered what was happening? Is that why she was murdered? Was she killed by the poisoner?

But what would Lady Li do now? She had to stop the empress from eating her food, that was certain. But how could she do that without revealing why she was there? And if the empress stopped eating, or if she ordered an investigation to find out who was poisoning the food, the killer could flee. She had to find a more covert way to find out who was behind the poisoning. She needed help.

She wanted to approach Te-hai, but what if he was behind the poisoning? Would he have a reason to want the empress dead? The more she thought of it, the more she realized that she was no closer to finding out who was poisoning the empress or who had stabbed Suyi. She at least knew more about what had happened, but not why or who could be behind it.

Lady Li returned to her rooms and called Eunuch Jinxi and Chu to her. Maybe they could help her.

After she explained that the empress's black blood meant that the empress was being poisoned, both of her servants appeared rightfully horrified.

"Oh, Mistress Li!" Chu exclaimed. "That is horrid! How would anyone even know how to make such a terrible drug?"

"I thought it was just a legend," Lady Li said. "I never imagined people actually made it and used it."

"Humans can be quite cruel, to each other and to lower creatures," Eunuch Jinxi said with a level of knowing wisdom well above his years.

"You both are bound to hear the palace gossip," Lady Li said. "Is there anyone in the palace who would want to kill the empress?"

"I think the empress has many enemies, my lady," Eunuch Jinxi said. "Both within the palace walls and outside them. She breeds discontent among her ladies. Sometimes intentionally, sometimes accidentally. One cannot be the sole woman in charge and not invite contention."

"But what of outside the palace?" Lady Li said.

"She is a woman," Eunuch Jinxi said. "Do men who

desire power need another reason to hate her and want to see her dead?"

"But she is the empress," Lady Li said. "The mother of the Son of Heaven. To kill her would be a crime against nature, against order, against the emperor, against China."

"According to many scholars, letting a woman rule over men is a crime against nature, Lady Li," Eunuch Jinxi replied.

"But she is a good ruler," Lady Li replied. "She ended the Taiping Rebellion, opened trade with the Western powers, and expanded the empire to the western regions. The country is at peace and is prospering, moreso than it has in a hundred years."

"And think about how much more China would shine if a man was at the helm," Eunuch Jinxi said.

Lady Li shook her head. She understood what Eunuch Jinxi was saying. For a woman to head the country was a perversion of Confucian principles. "A woman ruler is like a hen crowing," the Confucian scholars liked to say. And while the five relationships—a ruler over his subjects, a parent over his children, a husband over his wife, an older sibling over a younger sibling, and equal friendships—might make sense in the grand scheme of things or in the home, in all practicality the empress was the ruler, at least for now. Could the men not be patient? The little emperor would come of age in only a few years. Then the empress would step aside and nature would be righted. Killing the empress now, while the boy still needed a regent, was foolish and could plunge the country into war and recession. Besides, she wasn't the only regent. There was also Prince Kung. If something happened to the empress, he would be the most likely successor until the emperor could rule on his own. Was Prince Kung also in danger? Was Prince Kung...behind the poisoning?

Lady Li put her hand to her mouth. She felt sick again. Not Prince Kung. No, it couldn't be. If he wanted power, he could have taken it seven years ago when they staged the empress's coup. He could have citied Confucian principles to make himself the sole regent. Or he could have killed the empress instead of letting her take the regency. There were plenty of opportunities. But he didn't. He helped the empress overthrow the ministers her husband had put in place. Lady Li had been the one to carry their messages back and forth. Together, they were joint conspirators. Together, they risked their lives to put the empress on the throne. They were all bound by that decision for the rest of their lives. He couldn't, he wouldn't, betray her now. If anything, Prince Kung was the only man the empress could trust.

"Tell me about the court ministers," Lady Li said to Eunuch Jinxi. "Are there any who dislike the empress enough to want her disposed of? Are there any who would benefit from her death or removal?"

"Since the regency would only pass to Prince Kung until the little emperor takes the throne, there are few who would benefit from such a change," he explained, confirming her suspicions. "However, there is Minister Song."

"What about him?" Lady Li asked.

"He is...not gentle when speaking to the empress. He doesn't quite treat her with due deference."

"Who exactly is this man?" Lady Li asked.

"He is a second-rank minister, my lady. He has not been on the council long. His appointment was suggested by Prince Chun, Prince Kung's younger brother. Prince Chun is married to the empress's younger sister."

"Would Prince Chun have any grievance against the empress? I didn't know him well when I was here before; he was only a boy then. He is still quite young, correct?"

"Only in his early twenties, I believe. I do not think he would have an issue with the empress. Marrying her sister was a great honor. He has been working hard with Prince Kung and some of the other senior ministers to rise up in the court. But being the younger brother of an emperor and the younger brother of Prince Kung, the shadow of his elders might be impossible for him to escape."

"Do you know why he would have put forth this Minister Song for appointment?"

"No, my lady, not off the top of my head," Eunuch Jinxi replied. "But I can try to find out. See what their relationship is and find out how the minister feels about the empress."

"Minister Song..." Lady Li mused out loud. "His daughter is one of the empress's ladies-in-waiting, correct?"

"Yes, my lady," Eunuch Jinxi answered.

"How is their relationship?" she asked.

"They seem to have a mutual dislike of one another. I don't know if there is a reason for their animosity or if they simply do not get along."

"See if you can learn more about her as well. She might be involved. She would be close enough to the empress that she could be the poisoner." Lady Li then turned to Chu. "Do you have any information about the jewels?"

"Yes, my lady. A eunuch in the Ministry of Domestic Affairs was willing to speak with me, for a price. Eunuch Jingxi gave me the money for the bribe from your housing allowance. He said that there was a blue hairpin that the description matched the jewels I showed him. He said it was registered with Lady Kwan."

"Lady Kwan!" Lady Li gasped. "Is he sure?"

"Yes, my lady," Chu said. "Quite sure. He has the records to prove it. It must be Lady Kwan."

"But...why?" Lady Li asked. "What would her motive be? And you saw the strange way she acted when we visited her."

"Maybe she was acting that way because she committed the murder," Chi said. "Only a crazy person would kill someone in her own garden."

"I...suppose," Lady Li said, but she wasn't so sure. She was certain that the killer would be more calculating than that. But it would explain why Lady Kwan claimed she did not hear or see anything that night even though it happened so near her home.

"But there is still no motive," Lady Li said.

"If we look at her more closely, we may find one," Chu said.

18

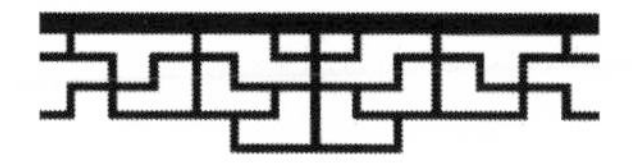

Inspector Gong was not a member of the court. Even though he had some contacts, like Prince Kung, he was unfamiliar with most members of the court and the court's inner workings. At least he had narrowed his search. Perhaps Prince Kung would have some idea of which of the second-tier ministers would want to poison Suyi.

A maid led Inspector Gong to the central courtyard of Prince Kung's mansion. A crowd of people—women, children, maids, eunuchs, and other visitors—had crowded around the periphery. Even though Inspector Gong came from a moderately large family, it was shocking to him how many people lived in Prince Kung's home. He made his way through the crowd and realized what everyone was watching—especially the women.

Prince Kung was sparring with a martial arts master. The prince was not wearing a shirt and his muscles shimmered in the midday sun. Even though the prince had not served in a military capacity for years, he was still in prime fighting form and was widely respected for his fighting skills.

The martial arts master and Prince Kung were circling one another, each getting a sense of the other's skill. The master made the first move, quickly striking with his right fist. The prince easily deflected the attack, spun around, and struck the master in the back. The crowd clapped.

The master did not stumble, but immediately found his feet and turned to face his opponent again. The prince did not waste time, but leaned back and kicked toward the master's face. The master bent back, avoiding the attack, but the prince then dropped down and swung his leg around, knocking the master off his feet, sending him to the ground flat on his back. The crowd cheered.

The prince hovered over his prone victim, and the master laughed. The prince helped him to his feet and clapped him on his back. The fight was simply a friendly match, and the prince had easily won.

The crowd started to disperse, so Inspector Gong approached the prince. One of the prince's wives was helping him towel off. She was a pretty girl, but a bit young for Inspector Gong's taste. She must have been a new wife, one that was clearly smitten with the prince since she giggled every time the prince looked at her.

"Ah, Inspector Gong!" the prince said upon seeing his friend. The two clasped arms. "Have you come to test your skills against the great Master Wong?"

"I fear I am a bit out of practice," the inspector replied.

"You should spar with me," the prince said as his wife placed a thin robe around his shoulders. "You never know when you will have to come to the defense of a fair maiden." He looked at the young woman as he spoke and wiggled his eyebrows at her. She could not control her giggling and nearly tripped over her own feet as she respectfully backed away and then ran from the courtyard.

"She seems sweet," the inspector said.

The prince shrugged. "A pleasant enough bedmate, and she is eager to please. For some reason certain men at court still think that tying themselves to me through marriage might benefit them in some way. I do my best to disillusion them of the notion, yet they continue to send their daughters to me in droves."

"Are you not still influential at court?" Inspector Gong asked as the prince led him into his study.

"I don't wish to be. I have given much in service to the empire already," the prince said. He lounged on a large plush sofa as a pretty little maid served them tea. "China is in a good place. Peaceful, prosperous. There are always tensions with the foreigner powers, but even they seem content, for now. It is time for me to pursue the things that give me pleasure, before I am too old or there is another catastrophe."

"And what are you pursuing, friend, aside from lovely women and good wine?" asked the inspector.

"I want to start a university," he said. "I want to found a school that teaches our people all the best learning the world has to offer. English, philosophy, science."

"You mean give men something to study besides the eight-legged essay? The old teachers or the men who reached power following the old way won't like it very much."

"Bah!" the prince scoffed. "The old men are just that. This is a new, modern age. And the empress supports my ideas. She also sees this as a time of change. She wants to start sending students to America and England, and then bring them back and give them court positions. And not just men. She wants to open schools for girls."

"A school for girls!" The inspector laughed. "What can girls learn in a school that they can't learn at home?"

"Anything a boy can learn. Sometimes men die and women have to take their place. Just look at the empress. How much more capable would she be while she is on the throne if she had been given any sort of education? It happens all the time. Look at Lady Li. She has to manage her own household, and she has only girls as well. Shouldn't they be able to manage their own affairs? They could be helpers for their husbands instead of just dependents who drain their resources."

"This sort of modern thinking can't be making you any friends at court," the inspector warned.

"I care not," the prince said. "I am officially the regent. I'm the highest ranking man in the country, next to the little emperor. What can they do to me?"

"But what of your sister-in-law?" he asked. "The empress is in a precarious state. I am sure there are ministers who would want to cast her off the throne and put you in her place."

"I don't think so," the prince said. "I wouldn't throw my weight behind any coup against her. And since I am the regent, who else would they get to take her place? No one."

"What if she were killed?" the inspector asked.

The prince sipped his tea slowly. "You are worried that whoever killed that girl could go after the empress?"

"Lady Yun was being poisoned. I have no idea why. Who would do that to a lowly lady?"

"You think her murder was an accident? Or a decoy?"

"I don't know," the inspector admitted. "But she was the empress's right-hand lady from what I have heard. If someone could get close enough to kill her, they could get close enough to the empress."

The prince sighed. "And you don't have any idea who could have been behind it?"

"Oh, I have an idea. What, you think I haven't been doing my job?"

"I honestly didn't think you would get very far. So tell me, who do you think it is?"

"What, and let you take all the credit?"

"You know you need my help. Why would you be here otherwise?"

"Maybe you should have been the detective," the inspector said.

"Get on with it!" the prince said, waving him off.

"I learned that a certain court minister recently procured some gu poison down Hei Mofa Street near the old temple. A second-rank minister."

"Which minister?" the prince asked.

"I don't know," Inspector Gong said. "That is why I need your help. Who are the second-rank ministers, and would any of them want to kill Lady Yun or the empress?"

"There are only three. Minister Jung, who has been serving since my father was still alive, Minister Huang, who is also old and doesn't leave his house much anymore, and Minister Song. Minister Song is about my age. He has quickly climbed the ranks. He was put forth and sponsored by my younger brother, Prince Chun."

"Why would Prince Chun do that?" the inspector asked.

"My brother is trying to promote himself, raise himself in the court. By promoting other ministers, they will in turn support him. It's all guanxi, connections, you know that."

"Would this Minister Song have a reason to harm the empress?"

"I don't think so," the prince replied. "It is clear he doesn't like her. He always disagrees with her. He thinks every decision she makes is a mistake. The empress is not above criticism. She even welcomes it if she thinks it can help her. But Minister Song seems to think it is his personal job to always point out her flaws and her weaknesses."

"Isn't that dangerous?" Inspector Gong asked. "If he angers the empress, couldn't she just demote him...or worse?"

"It's...complicated," Prince Kung said. "The higher men rise in the court, the more power they accumulate. More money, more friends. The higher a minister rises, the more difficult it is to demote him. Some of them even have their own armies."

"Is Minister Song such a man?" Inspector Gong asked. "Is he someone powerful enough that he could challenge the empress? Would he benefit from her death?"

"He can't rise any higher. Even if she died and I was made sole regent, first-rank ministers can only be princes, royal family. I don't know what he would get out of it."

"Does he have another motive? To help someone else rise or just to get a woman off the throne? What about your brother? Could her death help him?"

Prince Kung's eyes grew dark. "Careful, inspector."

Inspector Gong threw his hands up in surrender. "I have to ask. The empress tasked me with finding the killer. I think Lady Yun was an unfortunate casualty in a much bigger game. If the empress was the real target, then the killer had to be someone high-ranking, and someone with a lot to gain. The empress's death wouldn't benefit many people. In fact, it could cause more problems. There could be a fight for the throne or the foreign powers could nullify the agreements they signed with her. The empress's coup wasn't bloodless. A lapse in power is a lapse in control, and power always requires blood."

The prince shook his head. "You may be right, but what are we to do? This is all supposition. You don't have any proof. I can't just walk in and accuse my brother of trying to kill the empress. He is married to her sister!"

"Family members kill each other all the time. Most murder victims are killed by people they know, not a stranger."

Prince Kung put his elbows on his knees and rubbed his head in frustration. "How can you do this every day? It is maddening! You are never going to solve this case."

Inspector Gong sighed. "I appreciate your confidence."

"Maybe the empress will just lose interest."

"Lady Li won't."

"Oh, yes, Lady Li. We forget what started all this. You're right. Lady Li won't drop this."

"Have you been helping her in any way?"

"My spies are keeping an eye on her," he said.

Inspector Gong felt his heart drop. Did Prince Kung know he had been in the Forbidden City? Had been in her bedchamber? "Oh? And what have they observed?"

The prince smirked. "Wouldn't you like to know."

The inspector shifted uncomfortably.

"I know you were there, Anguo," the prince finally said. Inspector Gong swallowed. "How long has it been going on? Did you know her before all this began?"

"We only just met when I told her about Lady Yun's death," Inspector Gong replied, his mouth dry.

"You work fast," the prince replied. "I'm not going to tell you what you and she can and can't do. She is a gorgeous woman, and highly capable. You know I would have married her in a shot. But, and I say this as a friend, you are not one of us."

"So everyone keeps reminding me," the inspector said.

"I mean it," the prince said. "If it gets out, her reputation would be ruined. Not only because she is not a chaste widow, but also because she laid with a Han. The disgrace would be...well, she would never recover. Her daughters would never recover. Right now, both of her girls are on the short list of consorts for the little emperor. They would be ruined if what their mother did got out."

"Why do you care so much?" the inspector asked. "What exactly does she mean to you?"

"You don't work together to overthrow a government and not develop feelings," the prince replied. "It was a...passionate time."

"You...you loved her?" Inspector Gong asked, his mouth agape.

"Shocking, I know," the prince replied. "I don't even love my own wives. They are pleasant enough, but...you know how it is. Marriage is just an arrangement, nothing more. But Lady Li, yes, I loved her. I was furious when I found out her family wouldn't let me take her as a wife. We were so certain that we would be together after the coup. But it was not meant to be. At least the man she had been betrothed to had been a close friend, so I was able to make sure she was taken care of. Then the poor bastard went and he got himself killed. And now here we are. A woman like that shouldn't spend the rest of her days alone. I won't judge her for taking a man to her bed. She is still young. But you...you better be careful. If any harm comes to her or her children because of you...I *will* kill you."

The inspector paused for a long time. He was shocked at the prince's words. There was a lot of history between Lady

Li and Prince Kung, perhaps more than he could ever know or should want to know. He was amazed that she could engender such passion, such loyalty from a man. No. Actually, he wasn't. He was passionate about her as well. Had he not risked his own life by bedding her in the heart of the Forbidden City? He had lost his senses. But he would be loyal to her. He would never hurt her. He would do all he could to protect her. He had to solve this case, for her.

"I would never intentionally hurt her," the inspector said cautiously. "She...it was her idea for me to stay in her room that night. Not that I objected. But I didn't take advantage of her in her grief, if that is what you are worried about. And I would never reveal what happened. I care for her a great deal."

Prince Kung laughed and waved him away. "You could never take advantage of her. That woman knows her own mind and only does exactly what she wants. You know her better than that. If she wanted to sleep with you, my friend, you didn't stand a chance."

"We have to solve this case and get her out of that palace," the inspector said. "She is in danger every minute she is in there."

"I agree," the prince said. "Tell me what we must do."

19

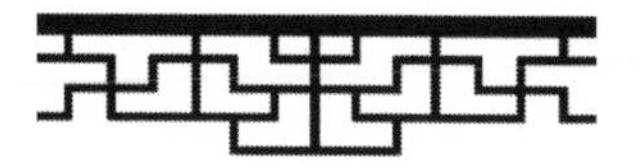

Lady Li paced in her chambers. She had to protect the empress from the poison without alerting the assassin. There simply was no way to avoid alerting the empress to the danger. In fact, maybe the empress would be willing to help Lady Li in her investigation. The empress was no stranger to danger and espionage, and they were friends. Surely the empress would understand. Lady Li shored up her courage and went to see the empress.

She had Chu prepare a bowl of simple broth so they could be sure no poison was added to it, then she carried the bowl to the empress's palace. When Lady Li entered the empress's sitting room, she noticed that the empress did not look well. Her eyes were closed and her skin seemed a sickly shade of green. Lady Li had a flash of panic. What if it was too late to warn her? She would never forgive herself.

One of the court ladies was massaging the empress's forehead and another was fanning her. Another lady was sitting over to the side by herself working on her embroidery. That third woman must have been Lady Song, the daughter of Minister Song. Who else would be minding her own business while the empress was obviously in distress? She must have despised the empress as much as her father did.

Lady Li walked over and took the empress's hand. "My lady," she whispered. "You look unwell. May I help you eat something?"

The empress opened her eyes and grimaced. "Oh, I feel terrible. I couldn't eat anything."

"I prepared this myself, my lady," Lady Li said. "I am sure you will feel better after you eat it."

The empress shook her head. "I couldn't..."

Lady Li nodded and put the bowl down. She spoke up so all the ladies in the room could hear her. "Ladies, this room is so drab. No wonder the empress is in a poor state of mind. Head out to the garden and pick some of her favorite flowers to brighten this room."

The empress did not object and the ladies filed out of the room. Lady Li then turned back to the empress and spoke in low tones. "My Empress," she said. "My dear friend, I need you to listen to me. Yesterday, after I ate with you, I got terribly ill. I think there is something wrong with your food."

The empress opened her eyes wide. "What did you say?" she asked.

"I'm sorry to tell you like this, but the fact that you are also ill concerns me. That is why I brought you broth I made myself. I believe the food from your kitchen is tainted."

"What!" the empress shrieked as she tried to stand. "I'll...I'll kill them...all of them!" She stumbled and Lady Li helped her to sit back down.

"Please, my lady, you must be calm. We don't want the

person poisoning you to know that we know. We must catch the person out!"

"I'm going to be sick!" the empress cried. Lady Li grabbed a nearby basin and held it while the empress vomited.

"How?" the empress asked between retches. "How? I have several tasters. And the leftover food is sent to the servants. How did this happen? Who else is sick?"

She made an excellent point. The imperial kitchens employed several tasters, and the empress only ate a small portion of the food. There had been no other reported deaths, but it was possible that some of the servants had gotten sick. No one would report such a thing to the empress. Any ill servant would just be replaced. But if the only food that was poisoned was something that just the empress would eat, someone could easily dispose of that dish instead of distributing it.

"I will find out if anyone else is sick," Lady Li said. "But for now, you must stop eating the food. But you can't be obvious about it. If the poisoner thinks you suspect, he will flee and we will never find him. Same with whoever is helping him. The tasters are probably being bribed, as is whoever clears the dishes away and distributes them."

"This is impossible!" the empress said. "Who would do this?"

"I don't know," Lady Li said. "Just be glad we discovered it before it was too late. Now we can find out who it is."

"And have him put to death!" the empress spat.

Lady Li nodded. "Of course, Your Majesty." She had forgotten that the empress could be ruthless when needed.

"Hand me your broth," the empress said. "At least I can trust you."

"You can always trust me, Your Majesty," Lady Li said.

"Can I?" the empress asked as she sipped at the broth. "When you haven't been completely honest with me since you arrived?"

Lady Li froze, unsure of how to answer.

"Don't stare so stupidly," the empress said. "It doesn't become you. What I want to know is why you didn't let me in on your little scheme in the first place. If you wanted to find out who killed Lady Yun, why didn't you come to me first?"

Lady Li sighed. "I hope you can forgive me," she said. "I hope you are not angry."

The empress tilted her head. "Do you really think me so petty? Do you think I could rule a country this large if I spent my days brooding over every perceived slight?"

"You are my friend," Lady Li said. "I didn't want you to think I only came to the palace for Lady Yun, and not for you."

"Women are never so simple. We always have many reasons for acting, never just one. If you came here to comfort me and find out who killed Lady Yun, how could I be angry?"

"I suppose I have been away so long, I forgot just how reasonable you are."

"Ha! I think you have been reading too many of those libelous newspapers. The ones that say I am full of passion and too stupid to rule. The ones that call for me to be ousted immediately."

"I never read those things," Lady Li replied, but she knew the papers existed. Indeed, there were even members of the court who didn't want the empress on the throne. Even though she was in the best position to rule, some would not be satisfied until she was living in a convent under lock and key. "How did you know?" she asked.

"I have spies everywhere," the empress said. "You and the inspector were not as inconspicuous as you think, sneaking around the other night."

Lady Li blushed. Did the empress know that she slept with Inspector Gong? Did she know that she saw her with Te-hai?

"So the inspector used you to investigate from inside the Inner Court," the empress stated. "He really is quite clever. I honestly didn't know how he would do it."

"He was in a difficult situation," Lady Li said.

The empress nodded. "I know, but what could I do? I couldn't allow him inside. The scandal would have been irreparable! I never would have heard the end of it from the ministers."

"But now he can solve the crime and protect the court," Lady Li said.

"But can he protect you?" the empress asked. "What of your little indiscretion?"

"I...I don't know. I hope no one else knows what I did," Lady Li replied.

"You trust this man so much? This man you just met?" the empress asked.

"I do," Lady Li replied, even surprising herself at how quickly she answered.

"Let's just hope he is worthy of that trust," the empress said. "There is no going back now."

"I believe he is," Lady Li said.

"Am I going to die?" the empress asked, suddenly changing the topic.

"My lady?" Lady Li asked, confused.

"You seem to think I am being poisoned, not that I just ate some bad food. Is it too late? Am I going to die?"

"I don't think so," Lady Li replied. "The poison was

being given to you in small amounts. I think that it will pass through your system over time."

"But poison isn't what killed Lady Yun," the empress said. "She was stabbed. So is her murder related to my poisoning?"

"That is the question," Lady Li replied. "Can you think of any reason someone would go to such extremes to poison you? Or would hate Lady Yun enough to kill her in a rage."

The empress shook her head. "It would seem that Lady Yun's death was sudden. The crime was instant and violent. You might not find a longstanding reason for it. No rivalry or intricate plot. She made someone angry and in the moment, they killed her. If you don't discover that immediate cause, you will never find her killer."

Lady Li sighed. "I suppose not," she said.

"On the plus side," the empress continued. "That person is most likely not a threat to anyone else, especially me. Lady Yun was the target of their anger, and they dealt with her."

"So you don't think I should keep pursuing this?" Lady Li said.

"I don't know about that," the empress said. "But the more immediate threat is who wants me dead. Lady Yun's killer will always be there, waiting to be found out. Whoever is trying to poison me could escape at any moment. Find the poisoner first."

"Are you ordering me to investigate this crime, Your Majesty?" Lady Li asked with a little gleam in her eye.

The empress nodded.

20

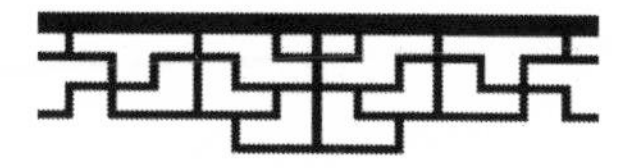

Inspector Gong was meeting with the eunuch in charge of the Ministry Household Affairs, Eunuch Liu. A note from Lady Li told him to find out if any servants had taken ill after eating leftovers from the empress's table, and a letter from Prince Kung gave the eunuch orders to comply with any of the inspector's requests.

"The palace has hundreds of servants," Eunuch Liu said. "You wouldn't believe the record-keeping that goes into running this place." He checked the labels on several scrolls before finally pulling a few from their storage shelf on the wall.

"Is everything that happens in the palace documented?" Inspector Gong asked.

"Everything," the eunuch said. "From how much food each lady eats to who cleaned their chamber pots that day. Each palace resident has at least one head eunuch, and then depending on how high ranking the lady is, she might have several more eunuchs serving her, in addition to a stable of maids. The eunuchs are in charge of compiling detailed notes on their lady every day and then sending the notes here, where the information is dissected and recorded again. It's a tedious process, I assure you."

"I believe you," the inspector said. "What happens to all the records over time? You have several hundred scrolls here, but from what you described, you must have dozens of records sent to you every day."

"Hundreds," Eunuch Liu corrected. "I am sent hundreds of records every day. I only keep the records here from this week. Then they are sent to the palace archives. Every few years the archives have to be cleared out because they get too crowded. Most of the scrolls from the Inner Court are just burned. No one cares what a bunch of ladies are up to day in and day out."

"Even if that lady is an empress?" Inspector Gong asked.

The eunuch shrugged. "I only do what I am told, inspector." Eunuch Liu opened several scrolls and quickly scanned them for the information he was looking for. "Hmm. Well, nothing seems out of the ordinary here. We had several maids that were unavailable because of their moon phase, but that's normal. The empress recently dismissed two of her maids for incompetence, but that happens with fair regularity as well. If they spill water she will have them thrown out on their ear."

"If a maid is dismissed by the empress, is she simply sent to serve someone else or is she removed from the palace completely?"

"They are removed completely," he said. "If the empress were to see the maid again, she would be quite angry. They are sent back home to their parents."

"With a ruined reputation?" the inspector asked.

"Usually," Eunuch Liu replied.

Inspector Gong sighed and rolled his eyes. So the killer

could be a disgraced former maid, but that would be too long of a list of people to narrow down.

"Come, come," the inspector said, rushing the eunuch. "Anyone actually ill?"

The eunuch continued scanning his notes. "Umm...no," he said. "That...hmm...well that is odd."

"In what way?" Inspector Gong asked.

"Well, just look at us. A household of this size, someone is always sick."

"Is it possible the list of the sick is somewhere else?" he asked.

"No," the eunuch replied. "It should be right here."

"So were the notes tampered with? Or the report stolen?"

"It was either stolen or never recorded in the first place. When the list of the ill was pulled from the other files that day, they just weren't listed or they were on a separate sheet and stolen."

"Is there a way to recompile the list?" Inspector Gong asked.

Eunuch Liu looked around the room at the stacks of scrolls and whimpered. "It would be...possible," he said. "But it would take time, a considerable amount of time."

"Probably more time than we have, you are telling me," the inspector said.

"Depending on how quickly the empress wants you to solve this case, yes," the eunuch said.

Inspector Gong rubbed his head. "All right, then tell me who could tamper with the notes? Who would have been in charge of compiling the information?"

"I have several scribes who help with that sort of work," the eunuch said.

"Can I interrogate them?" he asked.

"Perhaps," the eunuch said. "But..."

"But what?" the inspector asked.

"Ugh, you are so brutish. You are not a member of the court..." he began.

"So I have heard," the inspector replied.

"You aren't familiar with our ways here. I trust my assistants to do a good job, for the most part. But everything in here is for sale. Anything you could possibly want, from a piece of jewelry to opium to a night outside the walls to information to silence can be bought."

"So you are saying a bribe would be a better way to get information?" the inspector asked.

"Everyone in here has a sick mother who needs expensive medicine or a disgraced cousin who needs to pay off a massive debt. For myself, my dear sister's husband recently died and left her with four children to raise. Can you imagine?"

"So, for a price, you think I can find out who paid your scribe to tamper with the records?"

"Indeed," the eunuch said.

"Fine. Tell me which one of your assistants I should talk to and I'll find a way to get the information out of him, one way or another."

Eunuch Liu cleared his throat and cocked his head, waiting for something.

"Oh, shit," Inspector Gong said. "Not you too?"

"Did I tell you what happened to my poor sister?" he asked. "She has four of the loveliest children but her husband..."

"Yeah, yeah, yeah," the inspector said, reaching for a few coins in his bag. "Save the sob story and point me in the way of which assistant you think it is."

"Of course, sir," the eunuch said with a polite bow. "Follow me."

The eunuch led Inspector Gong to an adjacent room, this one also filled with scrolls, but there were also several desks where men were sitting, hunched over writing in new scrolls. They were extracting information from the scrolls and compiling it together.

"When the scrolls arrive," Eunuch Liu explained, "they come to this room and work their way around. This first fellow will see how much food the household consumed that day. By the end of the day, we will know how much food the entire palace consumed. That way we can make sure we are growing enough food on the imperial farms or ordering enough from other farmers. Or we can see if we need to cut down on anything the ladies are consuming too much of."

"That is impressive," Inspector Gong said.

"Quite," Eunuch Liu replied. "This next fellow tracks any textile usage. Silk, linen, rabbit fur, sewing needles, shoe forms, that sort of thing."

Inspector Gong nodded. He was somewhat familiar with the duties that went into running a household from watching his mother when he was a child. This was a household on an industrial scale.

"And on and on," the eunuch said. "Each man tracking different things. But this fellow," he said stopping in front of a desk near the end of the row, "would be in charge of noting any maids or eunuchs or residents who reported ill."

The boy immediately kneeled down and was visibly shaking from nerves.

"Stand up and look at me," Inspector Gong ordered. The eunuch did so, but kept his chin to his chest. Inspector Gong reached out and forced the boy to look at him. Well, he thought he looked like a boy but there was no telling how old he really was.

"Do you know why I am here?" Inspector Gong asked.

"You are investigating the murder of that girl," the boy replied.

"But why would I be talking to you about it?" the inspector asked.

"I...I don't know," the boy stammered. He had spoken clearly before, so the stutter made Inspector Gong assume the boy was lying. Inspector Gong just nodded and then turned to the rest of the scribes, who were all watching him.

"Why don't you all go get some fresh air," he said. Their chairs scraped the floor in near unison as they all quickly fled the room.

When Inspector Gong turned back to the boy, tears were running down his cheeks.

"Are you sure I can't beat a confession out of him?" he asked Eunuch Liu. "Look at him, he's about to crumble. Just a few slaps and he'd tell me everything."

The boy began audibly weeping. Inspector Gong couldn't help but feel sorry for him. He reached into his bag and pulled out a few coins.

"So who is this money for?" he asked. "Your sick mother? Disgraced sister?"

"My brother," he said. "My family is so poor that if I cannot make enough money to support them, they will cut him like they did to me."

Inspector Gong felt a small tug at his stomach. While being a palace eunuch did have some perks—a stable job with a good income—the loss of ever having a normal life was excruciating torture. Many Han people saw the practice as barbaric, just like the Manchu despised foot binding. He could understand why the boy would be willing to go to such lengths to protect his brother.

Inspector Gong took out a few more coins and put them in the boy's hand. "So who asked you to alter the records?"

"Alter the records?" he asked, confused.

"Yes," Inspector Gong said. "Who asked you to alter the records to omit anyone who has been ill after eating the empress's food?"

"No one," he said quickly enough that Inspector Gong believed him. "I admit that it was odd that no one has been sick lately, but when the weather is pleasant and people are not trapped indoors, illnesses usually abate."

"Then who was bribing you? And why?"

"Miss Chu, the maid for Lady Yun."

"Chu?" Inspector Gong asked, shocked. "What did she want you to hide?"

"She wanted to make sure that the blue sapphire hairpin jewel that Lady Yun owned was added to the inventory for Lady Kwan. I think..." He dropped his voice and leaned in as he spoke. "I think she stole the hairpin but didn't want anyone to know it was missing when they inventoried Lady Yun's belongings. I added the hairpin to Lady Kwan's inventory."

Inspector Gong began to pace. Lady Li told him about the hairpin. It hadn't been stolen, but was used to kill Suyi. But if Suyi had been killed with her own hairpin, why would Chu want it added to Lady Kwan's inventory?

She must have wanted to frame Lady Kwan for Suyi's murder. But why? Well, framing anyone would be better than getting caught. But did she have a reason for pointing the finger at Lady Kwan? And were the hairpin and murder of Lady Yun related to the poisoning of the empress?

Only Chu would be able to answer that.

21

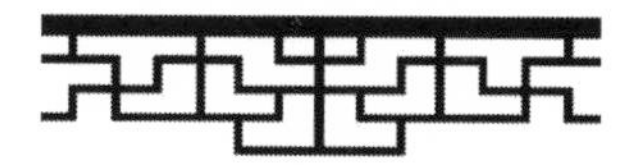

Lady Li returned to her room with a new energy. With the empress's support, nothing would stand in her way of finding Suyi's killer and the empress's poisoner. Maybe she would even solve the crimes herself, without the help of Inspector Gong. Wouldn't that just annoy him to no end. But where to begin?

She had to start with Lady Kwan. All the evidence—well, the only evidence Lady Li had—pointed to her. The blue hairpin had belonged to her. But was there a connection to Minister Song? There had to be one. Maybe Chu was right and it would only take a little more digging to find the connection and motive. She would go to see Lady Kwan under the guise of a social visit and somehow wrangle a confession out of her.

"Chu," she called out when she arrived back at her rooms. "We must dress our best. We are going to confront Lady Kwan. Chu?"

Chu did not reply.

"Jinxi?" she called. Still nothing. Where were they? It was not uncommon for servants to run errands, but for both of them to be gone at the same time? Someone should always be at the beck and call of a lady.

Well, they did have separate duties. And Lady Li was not a harsh mistress. She was perfectly capable of getting herself ready. That way she and Chu could visit Lady Kwan as soon as Chu returned.

Lady Li headed to the area of the room where her clothes, hair accessories, and shoes were kept. She would need to change her chaopao and shoes before heading out. She opened one trunk, but didn't find what she was looking for. Nor did she find it in the next trunk. She was about to give up since Chu was the person who kept everything organized. She would be able to find what Lady Li wanted without a second thought. But then another trunk, stashed in a corner, caught her eye. It wasn't one of hers. She pulled it out and lifted the lid. On the top was a chaopao that wasn't hers, but she knew who it belonged to. Suyi! It was the chaopao that she and Suyi had been working on together just before she left for the Forbidden City. But what was it doing here?

Lady Li lifted the chaopao from the crate, and as she did so she heard something clatter to the ground. Lady Li looked at her feet and saw a hairpin...a hairpin decorated with blue jewels. Lady Li picked it up and got something black on her fingers. It wasn't dirt, but when she held her fingers to her nose, she smelled the unmistakable scent of blood.

"Ai-yo!" Lady Li gasped. This was the pin that had been used to kill Suyi! But what was it doing here? In her quarters? In this trunk with Suyi's things?

She looked at the chaopao again and realized it was streaked with blood, but there was a large bloody area where the hairpin had been wrapped. Whoever killed Suyi must have wrapped the bloody hairpin in the chaopao and then stashed it in this trunk. But whose trunk was it?

She kneeled down and examined the other items in the trunk. There was nothing significant. Some plain silk flowers, flat soled shoes, and some very plain garments. Women's garments. Just then she realized that the trunk belonged to Chu. But why would Chu have the hairpin that killed Suyi? Was it possible that Chu had killed Suyi? And then wrapped the hairpin in the chaopao and hid it in this trunk?

Of course it was possible. But Chu? She was so young, and had seemed so sweet. And she said she had been fond of Suyi. Had it all been a lie? But what motivation would Chu have?

Lady Li rummaged through the trunk again, in case she missed anything. As she swept aside a handkerchief she saw what looked like a perfume box. It was small, round, and the lid was studded with tiny jewels. Lady Li picked it up, knowing full well that a servant would have no reason for owning such a thing. She twisted the cap, expecting to find a solid white sweet smelling perfume, but she found something much worse.

The substance inside was black as tar and smelled of death, a fetid combination of blood and other ingredients Lady Li had no desire to identify. Gu. This had to be the gu poison.

So Chu was behind both crimes? The murder of Suyi and the poisoning of the empress? But why? What motivate could sweet little Chu possibly...

"I didn't have time to hide it in Lady Kwan's quarters yet," a voice behind Lady Li said softly. Chu. Lady Li turned around slowly and saw the girl standing there.

"I was able to bribe the scribe to put the hairpin on Lady

Kwan's inventory, but I still needed to make sure you found it on her property somehow. I hadn't quite worked that part out yet. The fact that you found the jewels there had been a happy accident. I didn't realize they broke free in the struggle."

Lady Li stood and held the hairpin on her outstretched palm. "But why, Chu? Why? How could you?"

"It...I didn't mean to. I didn't want to. She...she caught me...I was...I was letting Eunuch Bo touch me. They like to do that, you know? The eunuchs. Even though they can't feel pleasure, they like to pretend. They like to look at us, touch us. It makes them feel like real men."

Lady Li shook her head in disbelief, but she remembered what she had seen between the empress and Te-hai.

"So that was how you snuck the gu into the empress's food, with the help of this eunuch."

"Yes," she said. "He was in charge of delivering the empress her food after it had been tested by a taster. But Lady Yun had followed me that night. She had been getting suspicious. I knew she thought that someone had been poisoning the empress. She had mentioned to me that the empress had appeared ill. So I had started poisoning her too. I guess she started to suspect me after she started feeling sick."

"But the poison didn't work quickly enough, did it?" Lady Li asked.

Chu sighed and shook her head. "I thought she had fallen asleep, but I guess she wanted to catch me. She followed me, she saw me. I heard her step on some leaves. I saw her. She ran and I chased her. She tripped. She fell out of those ridiculous shoes, so I was able to catch up with her.

"We struggled for a moment. I held my hand over her mouth. But then I grabbed the pin from her hair and I stabbed her." She struck her hand, as if reliving the moment, causing Lady Li to flinch. "I stabbed her again and again!" Chu said, punctuating her words with her fist.

"She finally stopped struggling. We were deep in the garden. It was dark and we must have gotten turned around. But I stumbled my way back to our quarters without being seen. I wrapped the hairpin in the first thing I could find, which was the chaopao she had been wearing earlier that day. I wrapped it up and threw it into my chest. Then I cleaned myself and went to bed."

"But why, Chu? Why were you poisoning the empress? Why take the risk? You have a good life here and..."

"Good life?" Chu snorted. "Do you even know why I am here? How I came to be a palace slave?"

Lady Li shook her head.

"I'm the daughter of the emperor!" she nearly shouted. "The Xianfeng Emperor was my father!"

"The late emperor? How is that possible?" Lady Li asked. She had to keep Chu talking. Where was Jinxi? He had to return soon.

"You know that all women who serve in the palace are the property of the emperor," she stated.

Lady Li nodded her head. Even though the emperor's consorts were usually chosen for him from the elite maidens of the land, he could have any woman he wished. It was not uncommon for a pretty maid to catch the eye of the emperor, who would then elevate her to the level of lady. That was why every woman dreamed of serving in the palace. Even a worthless peasant girl could rise to the position of consort if the emperor showed her favor, which was why all women in the Forbidden City, no matter their station, had to be Manchu. There could be no chance that a non-Manchu woman might find favor with the emperor and make her way to his bed.

"Mother said that the emperor forced himself on her. She said she had a sweetheart back home so she wasn't trying to get his attention like every other girl in the palace. She was only working here to save money so they could marry. But he saw her and was determined to have her. She fell pregnant with me. She couldn't return home after that.

"Her only consolation was that she would not be shamed. It was customary for the emperor to make her a rank seven lady upon the child's birth."

A seventh-rank lady was the lowest ranking lady, but it would at least ensure that the lady and her children would be provided for for the rest of their lives.

"But since I was a girl, the emperor did not fulfill his obligation to my mother or me. Mother always said that the empress was a jealous woman and would tolerate no rivals. Had I been a boy, the emperor would have to recognize me. But since I was a worthless girl, the empress told him to forget about me.

"When the emperor, the empress, and the rest of you nobles fled the Forbidden City when the White Devils attacked, most of us servants were left behind. Do you remember that?"

Lady Li did not confirm or deny Chu's accusations. She knew that many people had been left behind as they fled to the Summer Palace, but many servants had accompanied them as well. She had never given any thought to the people left behind.

"They were vile beasts. I watched as they brutalized my mother until there was nothing left. She died in my arms. I was eight years old."

Lady Li held her hand to her mouth as tears started to

fall. That would mean Chu was only fifteen years old. She was the same age as Suyi. She had no idea that the British had dealt cruelly with the slaves and servants left behind. She didn't know...

"I'll never forget that day," Chu said. "If the empress had allowed the emperor to recognize my mother, we would have been taken along with the royal family. We would have been saved. My mother's death and my whole wretched existence are because of the cruelty of the empress!"

"I'm sorry, Chu," Lady Li said. "I'm so sorry. I didn't know."

"You didn't care to know," Chu spat. "No one cared. No one asked. No one cared for me as the empress triumphantly returned after her coup and took the regency for herself. We were forgotten. I was told to wash dishes in exchange for my keep as the bodies of those who died at the hands of the foreigners were piled up and burned."

"I'm sorry, Chu," Lady Li said. "Truly. But...to poison the empress? For what? Revenge? What good would that do? Prince Kung would be regent and you would still be either a forgotten slave or an executed traitor."

"I'm the daughter of the emperor," Chu said again, but this time holding her head high. "With the empress out of the way, I could be recognized and given a high place in the court. If the little emperor—my *brother*—was to die without an heir, my children would be next in line for the throne and *I* would be the dowager empress!"

"Shhh!" Lady Li hissed. "Just to say such a thing is treachery! You cannot speak of the emperor's mortality."

"After everything I have done, you think I care about that?" Chu asked.

"But what now?" Lady Li asked. "You have been caught. I know everything. The empress will have you put to death."

"Not if I kill you," Chu said menacingly. She took a step forward and pulled a knife from her sleeve.

"You'll still be caught," Lady Li said. "Everyone will know that you killed me. They will then make the same connections I did. They will know you killed Suyi and poisoned the empress."

"You are the only person who has made those connections," she said. "And all the evidence is right there in your hands."

Lady Li looked down and saw that she was still holding the perfume jar of gu and the hairpin covered in dried blood.

"Everyone will just assume that whoever killed your hapless sister-in-law killed you too, but they will still be no closer to finding the killer."

Lady Li tried to still her heart as she realized that Chu might be right. She could kill her, dispose of the poison and the hairpin, and then claim she found Lady Li dead when she returned from her errands. Where was Jinxi?

"But wait," Lady Li said. "There is still one thing I don't know. The gu. Where did you get such a thing?"

"Oh, I got that from Minister Song."

"Minister Song?" Lady Li asked. "What does he hope to get out of this? He can't rise any higher."

"He can if I am proclaimed legitimate and we are married. As an imperial family member he would be a first-rank official. And if, somehow, our son inherits the throne, he would be the father of the emperor!"

"But why would he stake so much on you?" Lady Li asked. "Proving your position will not be easy,"

"He already has the proof," Chu said. "He found the details of my birth in the household archives."

Lady Li couldn't help but be rather impressed at how

Minister Song had so artfully arranged everything. If Chu succeeded in her plot, he could soon be the most powerful man in the empire. And if Chu failed, she would be the person punished. Lady Li doubted that she would be able to find any evidence of Minister Song's involvement in the plot.

But it was too late to save Chu. Even if Lady Li did stop Chu from killing the empress, she had already killed Suyi. No matter what happened next, Chu would certainly be put to death. Lady Li's only goal in this moment was to save herself.

"I am so sorry for the events that led you down this path, Chu," she said. "And for my part in it. We never should have left our loyal servants behind."

Chu gritted her teeth and her nostrils flared. She was not of a mind to be placated.

"But don't do this," Lady Li pleaded. "Don't make it worse for yourself. If you kill me, you will be caught. And the empress will make sure you suffer. If you let me go, I can plead mercy for you, as a victim of terrible circumstances and as a member of the imperial family."

"You would...try to spare my life, even though I killed Lady Yun, the girl you loved so much?"

Her blunt admission struck Lady Li to the core. She meant what she said, but she couldn't help but gasp at the pain that struck her heart.

"Y...yes," she finally said. "More deaths...more deaths won't bring her back."

Lady Li and Chu stared at each other for a moment. Lady Li tried to convey strength and warmth in her eyes. Yes, she was heartbroken over the death of Suyi, but she wanted Chu to trust her. Chu's death would not bring her peace.

Lady Li could not read Chu's expression. She seemed to be debating Lady Li's words and her own future. Should she cut her losses now and hope to live but never have a chance at the throne—the empress would see to that—or should she kill Lady Li and hope her original plan still worked?

"I don't believe you," Chu said.

She had opted for the latter.

22

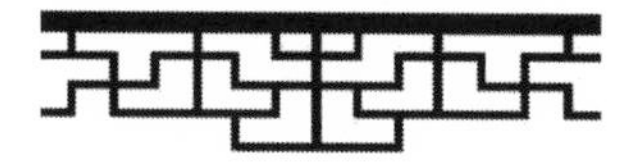

As Inspector Gong, Eunuch Liu, and several other men headed for Lady Li's rooms, they ran into Eunuch Jinxi.

"What are you doing?" Inspector Gong asked him.

He held out his basket of fruit. "Just collecting our ration of fresh fruit for the day, sir," he said.

"Where is Lady Li, and her maid Chu?" he asked.

"Lady Li was visiting with the empress, and Miss Chu was doing the laundry."

"Then hopefully Lady Li is still safe," Eunuch Liu said. "We can lie in wait for Chu's return."

"What is going on?" Eunuch Jinxi asked, looking concerned. "What is happening?"

"We are sorry, Eunuch Jinxi," Inspector Gong said, "but we think Chu might have been behind the murder of Lady Yun."

"What?" he asked. "But...but how is that possible? Chu and Lady Yun were friends. Chu is a sweet girl. She'd never hurt anyone."

"I am afraid we found evidence to the contrary," Inspector Gong said. "You should come with us. You will need to be questioned as well."

"Me?" he asked, trembling. "W...wh...why me? What have I done?"

"Just routine," Inspector Gong said, taking Jinxi's arm and leading him toward Lady Li's small palace.

As they neared the door, the men all heard a crash from inside, like a porcelain item thrown against a wall. They all looked at each other and then rushed through the door.

When they entered, they saw Lady Li and Chu struggling. Chu was holding a knife over her head in striking position while Lady Li was using all her strength to keep her from plunging the knife into her chest.

Inspector Gong moved to grab Chu, but he was too slow. In one quick movement, Lady Li's knees bent slightly, letting Chu think for a split second that she had won, but Lady Li then used the give in her knees to bounce back, throwing Chu off of her. She then grabbed Chu by the wrist and twisted her arm behind her back, forcing her to drop the knife.

Inspector Gong and the other men stood aghast, wondering what they just saw. Even though Lady Li had Chu in a firm grip, Chu continued to struggle.

"Don't just stand there!" Lady Li yelled to the men. "Help me! Arrest her!"

Inspector Gong motioned for two men to restrain Chu. They grabbed her by the arms and forced her to her knees. Inspector Gong went to Lady Li's side.

"Are you all right?" he asked.

"I'm fine," she said. "Just a little shaken. Please, don't hurt her," she said to the men.

"Let me go!" Chu yelled. "I'm a member of the imperial family! How dare you treat me this way?"

Inspector Gong looked at Lady Li with his eyebrow cocked. "What is she blabbering about?"

"She might not be lying," Lady Li said. "She claims to be the illegitimate daughter of the Xianfeng Emperor."

Inspector Gong walked over and stood in front of Chu. "Is what you say true?"

"Let me go!" she demanded again.

"You promise not to try and run?" he asked. Chu nodded. He motioned for the men to release her. She rubbed her wrists. "Go on, then," he said. "Tell me what happened. Why did you kill Lady Yun?"

"She already knows everything," she said, jutting her chin out toward Lady Li.

"Well, now I want to hear it," Inspector Gong said.

"Will you convince the empress to spare my life?" she asked.

"That depends on what you tell me," he said. "Just how high this plot goes. You killed Lady Yun, but were you also involved in the plot to kill the empress?"

"How did you know I killed Lady Yun?" she asked.

"You paid a eunuch in the Ministry of Household Affairs to have the blue hairpin added to Lady Kwan's inventory. You would have only done that if you were trying to make it look like Lady Kwan killed Lady Yun. Have you hidden the hairpin on Lady Kwan's property already?" he asked.

Chu shook her head. "She has it," she said, motioning to Lady Li again.

Lady Li reached down and picked up the hairpin by her feet. It was covered in what looked like black dirt, but Inspector Gong knew was dried blood that had been darkened by the gu.

"So, you were right," Chu said to Lady Li. "They would have caught me. I'm glad I didn't kill you. You are one of the nice ones. I'm sorry for Lady Yun too. She was kind to me. She didn't...she didn't deserve..." She held her hands to her face as she began to weep.

Inspector Gong looked to Lady Li, who was wiping a tear from her own eye.

"So you admit to killing Lady Yun?" Inspector Gong asked.

Chu nodded.

"Say it!" he yelled.

"I did it!" she screamed back. "I killed Lady Yun!"

"And do you admit to trying to kill the empress with gu poison?"

"Yes. I poisoned the empress. I hope she dies an agonizing death, worse than my mother did!"

"Anything else you wish to tell me? Anyone else you want to implicate? Will you tell me how you got the gu poison?"

Chu stopped crying and looked up at the inspector. "If I tell you everything, will you spare my life?"

"Unfortunately, that is not up to me," he said. "As a member of the Inner Court, the empress has the final say over what will happen to you."

Chu scoffed. "Of course she does. The empress holds the life and death of every person in this country in the palm of her hand, doesn't she? Well, I'd not give her the satisfaction!"

"Stop!" Lady Li yelled as Chu reached down and grabbed the knife she had dropped earlier. Before anyone could react, Chu stabbed herself in the neck, sending a stream of blood down her chest.

Inspector Gong grabbed the knife and held his hand to her throat, but it was too late.

Lady Li ran to Chu's side, taking the girl in her arms as she collapsed. "No! Chu, no!" she wailed.

"I...I meant it..." Chu whispered to Lady Li. "I'm sorry..."

23

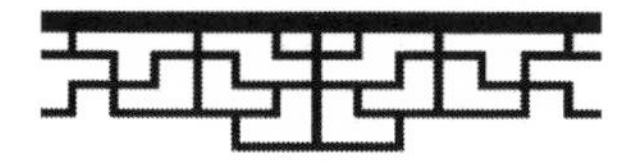

"Chu?" the empress asked. "Who is Chu?"

Lady Li looked down, unable to concentrate on what was being said around her as she could not stop seeing the blood that drenched her clothes and hands. Even though Eunuch Jinxi had washed the blood away and had put Lady Li in a new chaopao, the image of the blood in her hands and the girl dying in her arms was seared into her eyes.

Inspector Gong was attempting to explain to the empress what they had pieced together about Chu and how she was responsible for both Suyi's death and the empress's poisoning, but it was all gibberish to Lady Li. *How could this have happened?* she wondered. Of course, Lady Li had not been in the Forbidden City when Chu killed Suyi. She could not have seen any warning signs. But could she have saved Chu? Not that it would have mattered. If Chu hadn't killed herself, the empress certainly would have seen it done. Chu must have known that. It had to be why she took her life. She would rather leave this world by her own hand than at the whim of the empress.

"Lady Li!" the empress screamed, jarring her from her thoughts.

"What?" Lady Li asked. "I...I'm sorry. What?"

"The kitchen eunuch!" the empress stated, as if she was repeating herself for the umpteenth time. She probably was. "What was his name?"

"I...I don't know," Lady Li stammered, trying to recall what the empress was talking about. She held her hand to her forehead, but then quickly jerked it back, afraid of smearing the blood on her face, only to remember that her hands had been washed already.

Inspector Gong leaned over and softly said, "The boy who was sneaking the poison into the empress's food. Did Chu name him?"

"Oh, that eunuch," Lady Li said, her mind clearing as she looked at Inspector Gong's kind and calm face. "I...I don't...umm...oh, Bo. She called him Bo."

"Find him," the empress said to no one in particular, but two guards and some eunuchs immediately left the room. "He will pay for what he did. Death by bastinado," she screamed after the guards.

No one argued with her. After all, he did slip the poison into the food. He would be executed without trial. A death by bastinado meant he would be beaten with a cudgel until he was dead. It was a prolonged and painful way to die but was a standard method of execution for a eunuch who deserved it.

"Who else was involved?" the empress demanded. "I want names!"

She was on a blood hunt. Deprived of the opportunity to kill the mastermind behind the plot, she would take down anyone else she could. While Lady Li had never considered the empress to be a bloodthirsty or violent tyrant, no one had ever gotten so close to actually killing her.

"Your Majesty," Lady Li carefully spoke up, trying to calm her friend, "killing more people will not make this right. What Chu did was terrible, but she is dead. She had been horribly wronged in life and..."

"*She* had been horribly wronged?" the empress shrieked. "How dare you?"

Lady Li shut her mouth. She was not in the right frame of mind to try and talk reason into anyone.

"That little wretch tried to kill me. She killed Lady Yun. Your own kin! The girl you raised. Do you have more love for that murderer than Suyi?"

Lady Li let out a sob she could no longer hold inside. Of course the empress was right. How could Lady Li feel such sympathy for Chu after the terrible things she had done? Why did she feel so guilty for Chu's death?

She felt a hand on her shoulder and looked up to see Inspector Gong. He then pulled his hand away—it was most inappropriate for a man to touch a woman who was not of his family—but no one spoke against him, not even the empress. The warmth of his touch slowly coursed through her, and she was able to calm herself once more.

"I believe Lady Li is simply in a state of shock, Your Majesty," said Inspector Gong. "Even though the young lady was evil and deserved death, seeing someone die in your arms is never an easy task."

The empress let out a long, exasperated sigh. "I know this situation has not been easy on you, Lady Li," the empress said. "I will forgive you for misspeaking."

This was the closest Lady Li would ever get to an apology from the empress, and she would gladly take it. The empress was also in a difficult situation. She was still feeling ill from the effects of the gu poison and just learned that an assassin had been living in her very walls. She had to cope with feeling sad, angry, and scared, and she had to mete out justice as well. It was a balancing act Lady Li was glad she did not have to attempt. Not for the first time was she thankful that she was not in the empress's shoes.

"So who else was involved?" the empress asked. "She could not have carried this plot out alone."

"There...was another eunuch," Inspector Gong said. "But he was not involved in the poisoning. Chu paid him to frame Lady Kwan for Lady Yun's murder."

"Arrest him as well," the empress said, and two more guards ran off.

"Please, Your Majesty," Inspector Gong said. "The boy was very cooperative. He is the reason I was able to solve the crime and get to Lady Li in time. I beg of you to show him mercy."

"Very well," the empress said. "I will sentence him to death by beheading. It will be quick and painless."

"Your Majesty," Inspector Gong interrupted again. "I must insist. The boy is not a threat and did not act maliciously. Dismiss him if you must, but there is no reason to put him to..."

"Would you like to be next?" the empress asked in a voice so low it was much more frightening than when she screamed.

Inspector Gong stopped speaking, and no one else dared to speak on the boy's behalf.

"Good," the empress said. "Anyone else?" she asked. "Was anyone else involved in the plot against my life?"

No one spoke up. Even though Lady Li wanted to implicate Minister Song, without evidence she could not do so.

"Very well," the empress said, standing. "Inspector

Gong, I thank you for your service in rooting out this threat. I will see to it that you are fairly compensated."

Inspector Gong kaotaoed. "Thank you, Your Majesty."

"And Lady Li," she said. "My dear friend. I release you from your service to me so you may return home and see to the funeral of Lady Yun."

"Thank you," Lady Li said, also kaotaoing.

"Please do not stay away so long again," the empress said as she walked off her dais and left the audience chamber.

Inspector Gong let out a long audible sigh. "At least that is finally over," he said.

"For you," Lady Li said as she stood.

"What do you mean?" he asked, standing next to her.

"As she said," Lady Li said, not looking up at him, "I must prepare the funeral for Lady Yun. I have not even told my daughters of their aunt's death. And I must make sure the funeral rites are performed in time."

"I didn't mean to sound callous," Inspector Gong replied. "I only meant that the crime is solved and we don't have to stay here a wretched moment longer."

"That is true," Lady Li said. "Except for Minister Song. Will you continue to investigate him?"

"I am not under orders to. I don't have just cause or access to him," Inspector Gong explained. "There is nothing I can do."

Lady Li nodded her head. "I see. Well, I should be going."

Inspector Gong reached out and touched her hand. "Wait. Will I see you again?"

Oh how she wanted to see him again. In this moment she wanted nothing more than to collapse into his arms. She wanted him to comfort and console her. She wanted to make love to him again. She wanted him in her life and in her bed. But she could not give in. She was still a lady and had her family to consider. Here in the Forbidden City, she had been given a taste of freedom, but now she had to return home, return to normalcy.

"You may attend Lady Yun's funeral," Lady Li said. "But other than that I doubt I will see you again."

She slid her hand from his and left the audience chamber even though it broke her heart to do so.

24

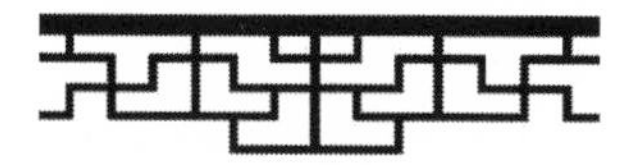

The chanting of the monks and the wailing of Suyi's mother could be heard from down the road. As Inspector Gong reached Lady Li's mansion to attend the funeral rites for Suyi, he was surprised to see a red banner hanging over the doorway. It stood as a stark reminder that Lady Yun and her family were Manchu to the end, not Han, who would have hung a white banner over the door.

The door to the housing complex was open to welcome mourners, but Eunuch Bai stood by, stoically watching each person who entered. He was dressed in white, as were all the other mourners. He entered the courtyard and saw the coffin laid in the middle, with the lid still open. In front of the coffin, many people were prostrating themselves to the young woman and to her mother. Lady Li and her two daughters were among them.

Inspector Gong took several joss sticks from a monk who was standing by handing them to mourners as they arrived. He walked to the foot of the coffin, bowed three times, and then placed them among the alter that had been placed there.

On one side of the courtyard was a large pile of clothes, money, food, and other items. Inspector Gong walked over and placed a beautiful pair of pot-bottom shoes on the pile. When the body was taken to the burial place, all of these items would be burned so the deceased could use them in the afterlife.

He then went to the coffin, situated himself behind Lady Li, her daughters, Concubine Swan, and Lady Yun's mother and prostrated himself before it.

The cries of Lady Yun's mother could make the strongest man weep. He knew the woman was ill and had now lost her last child. Her only family now was her daughter-in-law and her two granddaughters. It did not take long for the woman to wear herself out. She had to be carried away by several servants.

After she was gone, the mourners began to leave or talk among themselves. Since Lady Yun was so young and unmarried, she did not have many friends and did not hold a very high station in society, so most of the mourners were there to support their fellow Bannermen—as Manchu nobles were called since they were all descendants of the eight Manchu banners.

Eventually, Lady Li and her daughters stood up as well. When she turned and faced Inspector Gong, she seemed surprised to see him even though she had given him permission to attend the funeral.

Her little girls, who had always seemed happy to see him, looked exhausted and their faces were stained with tears. Even though Lady Li had had several weeks to process Lady Yun's death, her daughters only found out about it after she returned home after discovering her killer.

They were clearly heavily distraught over the loss of their aunt.

Lady Li handed the girls off to two servants. "I'll see to them shortly," she said. "Go ahead and get them ready for bed." The servants nodded and led the girls away.

"Inspector Gong," she said formally, with a slight bend of her knees.

"I am sorry for your loss, Lady Li," he said with equal formality. "I have information for you on the resolution of your sister's case. Is there somewhere we can speak, or should I come back later?"

She sighed and looked around. "We should get this out of the way," she said. "After we bury Suyi tomorrow, I would like to put this misery behind us as much as possible."

She led Inspector Gong from the courtyard and into a formal sitting room. She left the door open so that they could still be seen, but they were far enough away that it would not be easy for anyone to hear what they were saying.

"It was...so terrible," Lady Li said. "I'm so confused. I had already mourned her, but I feel like I am mourning again. But I do not know if it is for her or for Chu. I know Chu killed Suyi, but her life was so tragic. I can't help but weep for her."

Inspector Gong nodded. "Everyone grieves differently. And people are...complicated, to say the least. I think it is possible to be angry with Chu for her crimes and feel sad for the life she lived that caused her to do something so terrible."

"Did you speak to Minister Song?" she asked. "Will he pay for his role in the matter?"

"I spoke to him," he said. "But you know there is nothing I can do. We have no evidence of his role in the plot. The words of a murderous maid and a woman I met on the street are not enough to convict a man of his station. We don't have any evidence that he purchased the gu or knew about Chu being the daughter of the Xianfeng Emperor. I demanded that he give me the paper he found in the imperial archives, but of course he denied knowing anything."

"Did you at least tell the empress about your suspicions of his involvement?" Lady Li asked.

"I did," he said. "But she cannot demote him, not without evidence. But it will be a long time before she trusts him again, if ever."

"But is she safe with him at court?" she asked.

"I cannot say," Inspector Gong replied. "I think she is for now since he is being closely scrutinized. But who is to say he won't try something again, if he is as hungry for power as Chu said."

"And the empress will recover from the poisoning?" Lady Li asked.

"The doctors think so," he said. "It will take time for the poison to clear out of her system, but as long as she is not ingesting any more, she should recover."

Lady Li sighed and slowly blinked her eyes. "That is good. I suppose everything worked out."

"Do I need to do anything about Eunuch Jinxi?" he asked. "Didn't he recommend Chu for you?"

"I don't think so. He was recommended to me by Eunuch Bai, who cannot stop beating himself up over what happened. Eunuch Jinxi seems genuine in his innocence. He knew Lady Yun and Chu were friends, so he thought she would be useful to me. He had no idea of her involvement. I have no reason to doubt him. I don't want anyone else punished if there is a chance they are innocent."

She was certainly thinking of the other eunuchs who

had been executed after the empress learned of their involvement.

"After spending only a few days in the palace I remember why I was so glad I was not married to the emperor myself," Lady Li said. "The palace is a gilded cage. It is grand and opulent and a thing of envy, but the inside is rotten."

"I agree," Inspector Gong said. "I don't know how those women live that life every day."

"My daughters..." Lady Li started to say, but shook her head. "I don't know what I am going to do."

Inspector Gong remembered how Prince Kung said that Lady Li's daughters were both on the short list of possible consorts for the new emperor when he came of age. After this experience, Lady Li must have feared for their future.

"I have to ask," he said at the thought of Prince Kung, "did Prince Kung teach you that? How to defend yourself I mean? That was quite impressive."

Lady Li could not keep one side of her mouth from curling up in a smile. "My years as a lady-in-waiting were dangerous times. Yes, he taught me a few tricks."

He wondered what the other tricks were. He hoped he would have the chance to find out.

"Anyway, you should go before people start to talk," Lady Li said.

"I...I also wanted to ask, Lady Li," he started to say, but found himself stuttering. "About...well, about us..."

"Us?" she asked, confused.

"Yes," he said. "After the night we spent together, I thought maybe we...that I could see you again..."

"There is no us," she said firmly. "I am a Manchu lady while you are a Han nobody. There cannot be a 'we'. I must still consider my reputation, my future, my daughters' future."

Inspector Gong stepped back as if she had slapped him. "I'm not a nobody, *Lady* Li," he said. "I might not have a high and mighty title like you, but I'm well respected in this city, as is my family. I might not be a Manchu, but I am not beneath you."

"That remains to be seen," Lady Li said walking past him and motioning that he should leave.

Inspector Gong scoffed as he started to walk past her. What a cold, calculating woman. He had never felt so used.

"There can never be an us, inspector," she reiterated after he stepped through the door. "But if you were to call upon me again, I would not turn you away."

He didn't look back because he couldn't keep from smiling and didn't want to give her the satisfaction of seeing how pleased he was.

They both knew they would see each other again.

THANK YOU!

Lady Li and Inspector Gong return in *Murder in the British Quarter*, available now!

Subscribe to my mailing list so you never miss a new release!

AmandaRobertsWrites.com/subscribe-qing-dynasty-mysteries/

MURDER IN THE BRITISH QUARTER

https://amzn.to/2QlvnnJ

When a young Chinese woman is murdered within the British Quarter of the foreign legation, Inspector Gong is ordered by the Imperial Court to solve the crime before the incident escalates into war between China and the foreign powers. The only problem? Inspector Gong doesn't speak English. And he is hardly the type of man to be accepted by the British elite living in Peking.

Once again, he must turn to the one woman who can help him. The woman he can't stop thinking about.

Lady Li is trying to forget about Inspector Gong. He's a danger to herself, her position, and her children's future. But when he comes once again knocking on her door and asking for her assistance in solving a case, she can't resist, despite her better judgment.

Lady Li's language and diplomatic abilities allow her to freely enter the world of the Western visitors, but tensions between the foreigners and local people are increasing by the hour.

Will Lady Li and Inspector Gong be able to solve the crime without the answer leading China to war?

THE MAN IN THE DRAGON MASK

http://amandarobertswrites.com/dragonmask/

One Face

Two Men

And A Secret That Could Destroy An Empire

At the dawn of the Ming Dynasty, the emperor will do anything to ensure the future of his empire. Building the Forbidden City in fulfillment of his father's dreams is only the beginning.

But few people share the emperor's vision.

When a consort's betrayal has devastating consequences that rock the imperial court, the emperor discovers that the fight for the dragon throne has only begun.

ABOUT THE AUTHOR

Amanda Roberts is a USA Today bestselling author who has been living in China since 2010. She has an MA in English from the University of Central Missouri and has been published in magazines, newspapers, and anthologies around the world. Amanda can be found all over the Internet, but her home is AmandaRobertsWrites.com.

Website: AmandaRobertsWrites.com
Newsletter: AmandaRobertsWrites.com/subscribe-qing-dynasty-mysteries/
Facebook: https://www.facebook.com/AmandaRobertsWrites/
Instagram: https://www.instagram.com/amandarobertswrites
Goodreads: https://www.goodreads.com/Amanda_Roberts
Amazon: http://amzn.to/2s9QzAG
BookBub: https://www.bookbub.com/authors/amanda-roberts-2bfe99dd-ea16-4614-a696-84116326dcd1
Email: twoamericansinchina@gmail.com

ABOUT THE PUBLISHER

VISIT OUR WEBSITE
TO SEE ALL OF OUR HIGH QUALITY BOOKS:

http://www.redempresspublishing.com

Quality trade paperbacks, downloads, audio books, and books in foreign languages in genres such as historical, romance, mystery, and fantasy.

Made in the
USA
Monee, IL